DON'T LOOK BACK

SOE CIRCUIT FORTUNAE BOOK 1

THOMAS WOOD

BOLEYNBENNETT PUBLISHING

This book is a work of fiction. Names, characters, places, and incidents either are products of the author's imagination or are used fictitiously. Any resemblance to actual persons, living or dead, events, or locales is entirely coincidental.

Thomas Wood

Cover Design by Olly at MoreVisual Ltd.

Visit my website at www.ThomasWoodBooks.com

Printed in the United Kingdom

First Printing: July 2020
by
BoleynBennett Publishing

The Circuit Fortunae Series

Into the Storm (Prequel)

Don't Look Back

Playing with Fire

Close Quarters

Other series by Thomas Wood

Gliders over Normandy

The Trench Raiders

Alfie Lewis Thrillers

Before you start, have you read 'Into the Storm' the prequel novella to this series?

If you haven't and would like to, free of charge, simply head to:

ThomasWoodBooks.com/intothestorm

It's easy to download to all devices!

1

"Get back down there!"

I found myself standing at the entrance of the underground station, completely bewildered by everything that was going on around me.

"Oi! Bring me that stretcher! Now! Quickly!"

The bombs that fell seemed to do so in groups of four or five, a volley of incandescent rage and fury, only to be superseded by the next and the next. With every explosion came the knee-shattering tremor, that bullied me in such a way that I thought it a wonder that I was still standing on my own two feet.

Crump. Thump. Smash.

Miss. Miss. Hit.

I watched as the orangey glows of sunrise, which was not due for another ten hours or so, began to make ground behind the tops of buildings that surrounded this part of London. The furious swarm of wasps slowly trundled directly overhead, their tones one of terror and yet some sort of calming consistency. I listened to their pitch for a moment, trying my hardest to guess at their speed and altitude, but failing in the most miserable of manners.

The noise of the bomber engines was the only thing that did not seem to vary, for what felt like hours, the constant hum the only backdrop to the awful cacophony of noise that raged all around.

The bell that rang out, without ceasing, was only a part of my conscious mind, as the men of the AFS began their nightly appointment in hell. I watched as the men, boys some of them, leapt from the vehicle that they were travelling in, and began rolling out the insufficient hoses, that were apparently supposed to douse all of the flames that licked around the street corners and over the tops of the roofs.

There seemed like there would be no hope for this part of London.

As the droning engines began to rescind into the darkness, the screams and shouts of people, crawling out from every crack and crevice, got louder and louder, each voice wanting, *needing*, to be heard above all the others.

The bombs that screamed were due to miss me, but the one that was on its way to me was the one that would hiss. By the time the noise had registered in my mind as one of danger, it was already too late.

The young boys of the AFS were already buried beneath a pile of rubble and brick, their truck lying precariously on its side, with one man already screaming out to get the thing off his lower body.

I staggered around for a moment or two, a mouthful of dust and dirt settling on my tongue and a heavy application of sand-coloured ash sticking to the front of my body.

"Johnny! You okay, Johnny?"

I blinked enthusiastically two or three times over, as much as I dared, trying to flush out the dust caught in my pupils and to refocus my eyesight. I still could not see his face all that well, but I recognised the voice well enough. Besides, I was certain that he was the only chap around who would have known my name.

His voice, rowdy and over the top at the best of times, spat through into my consciousness as he repeated his question to me for the second time.

He had only been a few paces behind me on the stairs, tailing me ever since I had leapt up from where I was sitting and, decided to see for myself what was happening in the skies of London.

It was the first time that we had left one another's side for more than a few seconds in what felt like months, and within an instant, I had taken the debris of a one-hundred-pound German bomb to my face.

My ears burned so much that I found it almost impossible to distinguish the various sounds that were still so prevalent in the air. But the one that I could not force to one side was the ferocious crackling and roaring of flames, as they rose together, to grip onto anything worth burning, and vanquishing them in a matter of seconds.

"Can you hear me, old fruit? Are you alright?" his voice was quintessentially British, even in the face of all the chaos and danger that raged around us both.

I was mightily pleased that he was alongside me, as he had become an anchor to my wellbeing for the past couple of months, the storms of which would have threatened to shake many man-made anchors.

"Yes…Yes, I'm alright. Do I look alright?"

"You've looked unwell since the day I met you, Johnny. But, for you anyway, I'd say you look half-decent."

I found myself laughing wholeheartedly at what he had said, not because it was a witty putdown or hilarious quip, but out of an exhausted relief that, for now, I was still alive.

The falling bombs had slowed to a nothingness now, just the occasional thump many miles away as bombs were jettisoned or an unexploded ordnance suddenly ejected into life.

"Is that it then? Is that all they can throw at us?" Mike was almost ecstatic that we had survived our very first air raid. "If that is what they've been dropping on us then it was hardly anything to write home about, was it?"

"You'll be lucky, son," rasped a wrinkled face, as he lit a cigarette between his cracked lips. His head bowed slightly as he leant over the flame, revealing the letter 'W' painted quite hastily on his helmet.

He looked up at us both, inspecting the wings that adorned our rather dusty chests.

"Your lot need to buck their ideas up. Come up with something to stop them before they get anywhere near here. You understand me? Make sure you pass the message along…no one listens to the likes of us."

"We'll pass it along, mate."

"They'll be back. Might be five minutes. Could be two hours. But you can guarantee the beggars will be back. You'll see. Either of you two want a fag?"

"Go on then," muttered Mike, taking the box of cigarettes and accompanying matches. He had taken up the habit at the dispersal shed in Boscombe Down, and hadn't quite been able to shake the habit since. He seemed to think that the things were following him around, rather than him chasing them down.

"Why are they waiting?" I asked, received with a confused look on the warden's face. "Why do they wait? I mean to say that they know where London is, why wouldn't they send all their bombers over in one go?"

"Because," he muttered, removing the cigarette from his mouth, "them lot weren't dropping 'igh explosives. There were some in there I grant you, but mainly they was incendiaries that were coming down."

"So?"

"So…" he repeated, taking a hasty drag of his cigarette and appearing frustrated that he was interrupted again. "They let the incendiaries take 'old, then their muckers come in behind. London's ablaze like the Great Fire again. They can't miss."

His words hit home like a sledgehammer to my gut. If the devastation I had just witnessed was nothing more than a preliminary raid, then what we were about to receive was going to be all the more hellish.

"Michael," my voice was weak and pathetic, so much so that the warden didn't care enough to look up at me. Fortunately, Mike did. "Never mind. Don't worry."

Something had stopped me from saying what I had to say, but I could not quite pinpoint what it was. There was a chance that what I was about to say could have distracted us both from what we were meant to be doing, or even worse, he might not have cared whatsoever.

There was something in that momentary glance that he had gifted me, that had lasted for not more than two seconds, that quelled every fear that was harboured in my heart, and several others that were hiding away in other parts of my body. It was the same look that I had received from cockpit to cockpit as we stood on standing points, readying ourselves to intercept the enemy. All of which seemed so long ago now that it was almost irrelevant.

"Oi! You three! Gi'us a hand over 'ere would you? Got a family stuck down 'ere!"

"They dead or alive?" called out the warden,

tossing his cigarette to one side as if it hadn't been the most precious thing to him a few moments ago.

"One of 'em is alive. Not sure about any of the others. Just help, would you?"

To begin with, I stopped every time a shard of glass managed to penetrate my skin, the rose-coloured beads dribbling down my palms captivating me for seconds at a time. Before too long however, the beads were so abundant they could be ignored, the pain decreased and the ability to shovel away at the rubble with nothing more than my palms grew rapidly. Particularly after the first body was recovered.

The young boy, who was pulled from the pile of brick and dust that we worked on, could not have been more than eleven or twelve. His fringe was short and shockingly blonde, infused with a healthy dosage of greying dust. It looked almost as if he was sleeping.

There was no sign of anything untoward, other than the fact that the building he was sheltering in had collapsed all around him. For all I knew, he hadn't even heard the hiss as the bomb hit his house. It would have all been over rather quick for him.

His small, fractured body was laid out in what was left of the street, a warden's jacket hastily pulled over his upper body to keep him from the cold.

I thought that I would be stopped dead in my tracks at the sight of a child, perished, but in actuality it did nothing but spur me on further, to find the rest of his family so that they may be reunited in some backwards way.

I heaved at a burdensome lump of brick, a chunk of it still staying intact and clinging to what had been its former purpose. As I strained, I caught sight of a finger, just a nail at first but, as I let the brick tumble down towards the street, a whole hand came into view.

It was reaching up into the sky as if trying to gasp for air or find some source of light. I gripped it. It was still warm.

The skin was smooth and, despite a gushing wound from the palm, quite pleasant to the touch.

Tears rushed to my eyes as I gripped onto it, still no closer to knowing whose hand it was that I was clutching hold of, or whether they were alive or not.

"Over here!" I sobbed, as I pictured the young boy's sister or brother, in a similar state to their sibling.

"Alive?" called out another voice, one that I did not recognise.

Instinctively, I looked down at the small hand that I held in my embrace, willing it to give me some sort of an answer.

"Alive?" I whispered gently into the night, as a teardrop fell onto the young hand, washing some of the grime away.

At first, there did not seem to be anything, but then, as another tear fell onto it, I thought I saw the hand twitch. Then, I felt it, there was a squeeze. Whoever it was that was at the other end of this hand, was very much alive.

"Alive!" I belted at the top of my lungs, not relinquishing my grip in the slightest. "Alive!"

Carefully, the men around me began to pull gently at the surrounding bricks and debris, as if each one was resting on the victim's head.

I, on the other hand, refused to move. Whoever it was under there would need me, they would want to know that there was always someone connected to the outside world. They would no longer feel trapped or forgotten.

Then, as quickly as the bombs had fallen, a face was revealed, a timid, battered face. The bruises had engulfed her face quicker than I thought they could do, her features so swollen that I was surprised that the debris hadn't simply lifted from her head as they bulged.

Even with all the blood and bruises, I could tell that the young girl, no older than four or five, was in the possession of a captivating beauty. Her nose was small and unobtrusive, her cheeks, made worse by the swelling, puffed up so much that she looked like a balloon.

But it was her eyes, her deep green eyes, that I had locked myself onto. They were beautifully bright, so bright that the searchlights that scanned the skies seemed dull in comparison.

Still clutching hold of my hand, she was lifted from the pit that she was in and carted to an awaiting ambulance, which was already full to bursting with other casualties of the night.

As she perched herself down next to two elderly gentlemen, who seemed more frustrated that their night down the pub had been interrupted, she kissed my hand.

"Fank you, Mister. I'm going to tell my brother all about you in the morning."

"I know you will, sweetheart. I know. You stay safe now, okay? Promise me?"

"I pwomise, Mister."

I looked at her for a few more moments, before the tears threatened to roll down my cheeks and I was forced to turn away. I couldn't have anyone seeing a pilot acting in the way that I was.

"You okay, Johnny?"

"Yeah, I'm fine, Mike. But I tell you one thing."

"What's that?"

"That's the last time we visit that cinema."

2

Even as I sat in the middle of a scene of peace and tranquillity, the echoes of the past refused to leave my scarred mind, as I played the soundscape of times gone by over in my head, over and over again. They never stopped.

It was an unusually warm mid-October afternoon, especially when the recent weather was taken into consideration, and I took great joy from being able to sit outside, by the slow-flowing stream, throwing the odd stick and stone into its icy waters. It was warm, but not warm enough to peep my toes into, so I was more than content to simply dangle my limbs over the bank and wait for the summer.

It was a long time to go until the summer of 1941, but I could only hope that it would be far better than its counterpart of 1940.

As the sun began its final descent into the fragrant colours of the winter months, I allowed my eyelids to meet halfway, just kissing each other, like a long-separated couple on their reunion.

No, not now. Not here.

My lungs ached as I took a deep breath of Cornish air into my body, causing me to flinch ever so slightly. It still hurt, in more ways than one.

I ran my hands over the backs of my arms, gently caressing the skin that was slowly healing from its wounds. The inflammation was going down, but it remained as tender as if it had been burned just yesterday.

Somehow, the never-ending sound of water trickling its way around defiant rocks began to soothe me. It made me feel almost human again. I enjoyed its company, the way in which it was there for nothing but a fleeting moment, enough time to make me happy, before continuing on its journey once more. It didn't seem to hang around all that much. It was quite like my own life in many ways.

I let the noise filter through my ears even more, as the downward stream continued to work away at the sharp and jagged edges of the rocks that lay around its banks. I had long been fascinated by that kind of geology, the way that if a stone was to sit in the path of oncoming water for long enough, it would become smooth, almost void of any imperfections whatsoever. It was what I needed right now.

Go on, do it. Why not?

I pulled myself upright, forcing the reunited eyelids to part once more for the time being. It was okay, the two lovers would be in one another's embrace once again before too long, no matter how much I wanted them to stay apart.

It was four-forty in the afternoon. Plenty of time until dinner was served.

I looked back towards the house. No one seemed to stir. There was no movement around the grounds, no minute heads bobbing around in the windows. It was what had attracted me to this place when I had seen the advertisement in the local paper, despite what connotations it had attached to it.

It was an old, Victorian farmhouse, the grey-stone walls rising high over three floors, quite unlike any other building in the near vicinity. Its rooms were airy and large, with spectacular views over the surrounding fields, that greeted me every morning that I rose.

I got up earlier these days, about four in the morning, more often than not in time to watch as the infant sun began to peer over the edge of the horizon, as if enquiring as to whether it could rise or not. I enjoyed those times, when not a soul was awake themselves yet, when I had time to be alone, with my thoughts and memories, that no one else could mar. No more than they already were anyway.

I often took the time to consciously forget the dream that had haunted me, so often a distortion of the living nightmare that I was in.

Nothing could be worse than my life, I had frequently told myself, but it had seemed that my subconscious mind had wanted to go one better, night after night.

I had to make do with the smaller things in life now, forcing myself to enjoy the life that I now led. It was why, as I lay on the bank, that I began to smile as I listened to the mid-afternoon birdsong. The chirrups and chirps were enough to bring anyone back from the brink of death, all you had to do was simply listen to them.

Every once in a while, I would catch sight of one, up in the treetops somewhere, bouncing around on an unstable branch, as he called out to the rest of his friends about what fantastic luck he had in finding his latest meal.

Each tweet seemed to fight with the last for my attention, to the point where it felt as though I was sat in amongst the violas of a symphonic orchestra, as each member began to warm up in the most boisterous of fashions. It was all quite marvellous.

So marvellous that I decided to join in.

For a few moments, I was back up in the sky again, albeit at a considerably lower altitude, and not a single round of machinegun ammunition in sight. I ducked and weaved between the branches of the trees, darting around in an excitable fashion with the rest of my kind. I longed to be up there with them, with not a care in the world, other than where I might find my next worm.

But, within an instant, my eyes parted ways once more, and I was back by the stream.

It was still only four-forty. Plenty of time till dinner was served. It was such a nice day, after all, unusually warm weather for an October in Britain.

At first, it was just my toes that broke the surface of the water, yet another obstruction for the water to dance around but, before I could really think about what I was doing, I was lying flat on my back, the biggest obstacle the stream had seen for hundreds of years.

The water was cold, icy cold, so much so that I felt the little nerve endings at the tips of my fingers and toes begin to scream at me with all their might. The pain, eventually, began to subside, until it was nothing more than a gentle poke as the stream negotiated its way around me.

Maybe I would be able to get rid of my jagged edges and imperfections if I was to lay there long enough. It really would be an awfully long time.

As I lay there, beckoning the water to wash me, cleanse me of the thoughts that had plagued me for the last few months, I slowly began to take notice of the smell that infested this small part of the world.

It had the inevitable scent of dampness to it, the kind of smell that you recognise as you pull a sodden sock from the basin in front of you, instantly recognisable that it has recently been deluged.

There was a sweetness around the aroma though, one that forced the image of dirtied socks being washed in a basin away from my mind. It was clean air, the kind that I had so often craved as I sat irritably outside the dispersal hut, or down in the unwelcome embrace of a public shelter.

My lungs filled themselves once more with untainted air of the Cornish countryside, as I felt myself sinking further and further into the depths of the shallow stream with every desperate exhalation of air.

The canopy of trees above me seemed to enshroud my entire existence, allowing just enough of the mid-afternoon sun through its leafy blanket to remind me where I was. Every now and then, with a slight breeze that rustled calmly through the treetops, a brilliant flash of light would bounce towards me, smashing into my eyeballs and forcing them tightly shut.

The brilliance of light that cannoned its way towards me only ever reminded me of an empty gun, the pathway of light that moved its way to my eyes conjuring up images of the final few rounds of Hurricane ammunition, before I would have to find an alternative way to send my adversary to the ground.

There was a fleeting moment, as I lay in the stream, crunching my eyes shut on account of the sunbeam, that I resembled something that felt like being happy. Although, thinking back now, it was difficult to determine, it had been so short-lived, and it was now a feeling that was completely unknown to me.

As quickly as the feeling had come and gone, so

too had the light, which was quickly engulfed by some sort of devouring darkness.

I opened my eyes. Surely I had not been lying there so long that the sun had given up for the day?

Five twenty-three. Precisely.

There was still plenty of time until I would have to make my way back to the farmhouse. Dinner would not be until six.

It was the only focal point that I had of my day anymore; eating. Even sleeping was not much to keep time by anymore, for I rarely did it. Eating, on the other hand, was something that I had learnt to continue doing, the first few days after the incident characterised by insomnia and hunger. But soon, I learned that even a grief-stricken man must line his stomach. Otherwise, what would he have to throw up again later in the day?

It took me a while to notice the source of the darkness that had suddenly befallen me, robbing my body of the relative warmth of the sunlight and making the coolness of the water that much more cruel.

Mrs Philips stood on the side of the small bank, as she did her best to offer up a maternal look upon one of her deranged children. She had tried to understand my plight, truly she had, but there was still something about a woman who had had no children of her own, that meant that she was not able to fully comprehend my situation.

She still continued to try, though, with a sort of

pseudo-motherly love that only a fifty-something-year-old widow could offer.

I stared straight into her hazel-coloured eyes, the sort that saw everything that went on in a village, but accompanied with the good grace and reserve to keep her lips firmly shut. I knew that this little episode of me lying prone in her stream would go no further than the two of us. It made me feel more like myself again.

As I continued to loiter on the thought of what a nice woman Mrs Philips had been, her kind and patient character, especially with a man like me, I suddenly wondered whether she would have been as understanding if I had not been paying her weekly.

She was the owner of the old Victorian farmhouse, that was just about visible behind her greying head, the place where I had been staying for the last three weeks or so now. Telwyn farm was a place that would be forever in my heart, and I would be eternally grateful to the old gentleman who had surrendered his newspaper so that I could get a glimpse at the advertisement.

"I liked the sound of the water. It's gentle. Calm."

I thought I saw a slight smile try to flicker at the side of her mouth, before it returned to its steely glare, like a parent that wanted to tell her child off despite how funny the situation was.

"This is Mr Calhoun," she said, trying to ignore the fact that I was lying in a stream, fully clothed. "He would like a word with you…when you're finished."

It was only at that moment that I realised that the hungry darkness that had so quickly enveloped my existence had not been down to Mrs Philips alone. Of course, it couldn't have been, she was such a small lady after all.

Mr Calhoun too was a small man, only an inch or two taller than Mrs Philips, but his face was decidedly more unwelcome, as it seemed to slope to one side. If I had only just met the two of them, I would have said that they were the perfect couple.

"Andrew Calhoun," he announced, with an odd impediment that I couldn't quite place. "Detective Sergeant Calhoun, with the Cornwall County Constabulary."

"Oh?"

"I wondered if I might have a word, Mr Parker, Sir."

3

Before I could disembark fully and find my way off the platform, the area surrounding me was immediately awash with young children, screaming and hollering louder than a German bomber ever could.

I was thankful that I had finally arrived at Paddington station, in the heart of the empire, as it meant that I could say goodbye to the endless huffing, chuffing and squealing of the locomotive as it struggled its way from the west country. But now, as I waded my way through the sea of brightly coloured school caps and immature bodily noises, I wanted nothing more than to endure another four hours in the silent carriage.

I felt sorry for the children around me, even though they seemed mightily glad that they were on their way to the countryside. Many of them would never return home, I assumed and, even if they did, a lot of them would return to find one less parent than when they had departed. But even so, I could still feel the childlike excitement of being evacuated – a brand new adventure to be embarking on.

I thought for a moment of Mrs Philips, my mind wandering just ever so slightly to the old grey farmhouse and the pleasant surroundings. I tried to picture just two or three of the ruddy-faced children around me, out in the fields surrounding her home, before stumbling back in time for tea. Something told me that they wouldn't quite fit in there, nor would they be all that welcome. Mrs Philips didn't seem to enjoy the talk of children all that much, not to mention the possibility of living with them.

I made my way to the bus station, where I was due to hop on one of the old, ageing buses, only to be patronised by one of the conductors about how to get off the thing.

Just as I was about to leap onto the back of one of the swiftly-departing red vehicles, ducking my head down so as not to be soaked by the torrential downpour that was deluging this part of the country, I heard a voice, calling my name.

"I say, Parker! Over here, Johnny!"

Turning, I saw the familiar handsome and confident face of Michael Hope, the name suiting the man's personality to the letter. As he came closer, his features began to return to my memory; the glistening eyes, the smile so warm that you could dry your laundry by it. All in all, he was an attractive young man, irritably so.

"Mike," I breathed, almost completely out of any oxygen, or so it seemed. Within a flash, he had caught up with me, motioning us to both get under the nearest bit of cover, so as to escape the onslaught of the autumnal rain.

"Oh, look," he said, brushing some of the droplets from shoulders, with little consequence other than forcing it into the fabric. "This is fresh on today."

"Could have fooled me," I muttered, chuckling ever so slightly at his misfortune. "Congratulations, by the way."

"What? Oh yeah, thanks."

He twisted his wrists round once or twice, just to show off the thicker bands that now encircled them.

"Flying Officer," he said. "All I did was survive."

He looked down at them for a second too long, as if he was reliving every single man that had gone before him, their names ingrained on his mind forever.

"How are the other chaps?" I asked, innocently enough, trying to grab his attention on those who were still living.

"Oh, you know how it is," he muttered, rolling his eyes. "Can't wait to get away from Weald. You know, they seem to think that Boscombe was better. For some reason, they cannot remember how awful the beer was there. The pubs around Weald are far more accommodating anyway."

"You mean they don't charge as much?"

"Exactly. Barmaid's prettier to look at, too."

We continued to chat for another twenty minutes or so, as we negotiated the intricacies of the transport network, trying to find our way to the address printed on the card we had each been given.

As we talked, I watched Mike's fingers as they gently caressed the golden eagle that adorned the front of his chip bag cap. I had always preferred the chip bag, as if it added an element of boyish sedition to an otherwise immaculate uniform.

Mike had been wearing his, until we boarded the underground, at which point it found itself lying on his lap, where it continued to be petted and stroked by Mike's nimble fingers. There was something that the never-ceasing fingers were hiding, a tale or revelation that no amount of polite chit-chat would be able to keep hidden forever.

I had known it the very second that I had set eyes on Mike's face. There was something that was troubling him, behind his kind and attractive face, something that was even forcing him to ignore the odd glance of an admirer, that he customarily would acknowledge.

I was not able to hold it against him, however. I had gradually become accustomed to people hiding things from me my whole life, in fact, it had made me just as good at it myself. There were things that I was so good at keeping from others that I almost forgot about it myself.

Another few minutes slowly passed by and it did not take me too long to notice the small beads of sweat that began to form upon the palms of Mike's hands, in some sort of holding pattern and waiting for the signal to begin dripping to the floor.

It made me wonder how much longer he was going to hold it in. He was certainly gearing himself up so much I thought he would burst.

"Look, Parky..."

Here we go, I thought. Finally.

I was not naïve enough to think that what was about to head my way would be in any way considered as good news. Our country was at war, and I didn't think many people had had any good news for a considerable amount of time now. Perhaps apart from the owners of production companies that manufactured weapons and everything else that would see its demand fly through the roof over the coming months.

"Johnny, there's really something I need to get off my chest. I was rather hoping that I would see to it after this meeting, you know. I didn't want you to go all funny on me."

"Spit it out, Mike."

I felt no indignation or frustration with Mike as he continued to struggle with his words, but there was something that got to me about those few brief seconds. Mike had never had any bother before about getting the words from his head to his mouth, in fact sometimes he could have done with holding his speech up for a moment or two. It had landed him in hot water more than once.

"Sorry…it's just, I've been building this whole episode up in my head so much that, well…I had rather hoped that it hadn't been me who had been the one to tell you this."

"Come on, Mike. I promise I won't go funny on you. I'll buy you a beer if I do."

He looked up from his lap as if he had been so surprised to hear of my offer of a drink that he was half-hoping that I would have a funny turn.

"It's Teddy," he said, morosely. "Teddy Higgins."

He did not need to add the additional name on the end. I knew full well who Teddy was, and I knew immediately that he was dead. There was no other possible outcome to a conversation such as this one, especially not while we were at war, anyway.

Edward Higgins had flown with me during our time in the Volunteer Reserve, about six months before the outbreak of the war. We had become steadfast friends during that time, flying older planes like the Gloster Gladiator and some other antiquities that the air force managed to dig up from somewhere.

I knew what was coming next, but it still did not stop me from thinking back to the long summer evenings of cricket and drinking that we had so often enjoyed together, along with a few others who were now nothing more than mere memories, even in the minds of their own mothers.

Mike didn't seem capable of saying the actual words, "He is dead," or the like, but instead commenced the retelling of the tale that would only end up in one outcome for poor old Teddy Higgins.

"We were sent to carry out a patrol over Maidstone. Fifteen thousand feet," he added, as if it was of any real consequence to the story. Still, it set the scene. I could almost taste the moisture forming up on the inside of Teddy's oxygen mask, the perspiration already just lubricating his eyebrows in anticipation of what would happen next.

"We saw some 110s, heading north. Twenty of them. A real fish in a barrel scenario," Mike said, his face lighting up for a brief second before remembering the sobering conclusion to his tale.

"We had the height advantage and so swung round so that we could come at them side-on. It was pretty spectacular all told. We downed three of them just in our first pass, we had that long to hit them. Plus, their gunners couldn't get round to us, so we were almost perfectly protected."

As he told the story, I watched the eyes that were seeing all of the day's actions pass before him once more. I did not flinch as he recounted the events, but there was a sizeable portion of my being that was downright envious that I was not there. The rest of me was simply awash with pure guilt.

While the rest of the chaps had been continuously engaging the enemy, I had been hiding away in a funk hole, like all the rest of the occupants of Mrs Philips' establishment. I saw myself as no better than a conscription dodger.

"We turned back for a second run. But, looking around, I could see Teddy nowhere."

Mike turned his head away for a moment, to stare out of the windows of the underground into the inky blackness that glared back at him. I followed his gaze, watching his reflection intently, as he fought valiantly to hold back the tears that were now welling. He had cared for Teddy just as much as I had done, just as much as any of the other boys. He was a very likeable character.

"They must have been damn lucky," he crackled, as he eventually turned back to face me. The tears had refused to fall, but instead had sat patiently in his eyes, turning them a vibrant red colour. I wondered how he was able to see anything at all.

"He had lost height. Probably about four or five hundred feet below us. Lagging behind immediately. They must have hit the cooling tank as he was already streaming white smoke. I broke away to circle back towards him, just in case one of the 110s went after him.

"By the time I got alongside him, he was losing height and speed quicker than a boulder. The cockpit was full of fumes. I shouted at him, I told him to get out. But there was nothing, no reply."

He wiped away at his face as he was jostled around by the carriage, in much the same way that his whole body would have been convulsed and thrown around by the Hurricane.

"Then, he managed to get the canopy open. I

watched him carry out his procedures. He even managed to invert to get himself out. His little body flopped out and fell."

He paused, right at the moment where I wanted anything but silence.

"And?"

He looked up at me, "He kept falling. I don't know what it was. Whether he was overcome by the fumes. Or if his parachute failed."

My eyes bulged at the thought of one of my best chums dying in such a way. I couldn't imagine what it would have been like for him, nor Mike.

"Twelve thousand feet. No chute. Poor old Teddy."

I would have excused Mike for bursting into tears right there and then, but I got the distinct impression that he had engaged in many hours of tearful recollection since the fateful episode.

"They found his body just outside Tonbridge. At least they think it was him. He was a bit of a mess."

He stared at me, trying his utmost to determine the thoughts that were whizzing through my mind, but I was a wall, devoid of any human emotion. I had liked Teddy, loved him even, but the loss of him was of no real consequence to me. There was nothing that I could do about it now. No point in lingering.

"I was rather hoping to leave it for another hour or two, I'm sorry."

"It's alright."

"I just thought that you ought to know. No one

really wanted to be the one to tell you. You know, after what happened to—"

"I said it's alright," I said shortly, a few of the other occupants of the carriage picking up on my anger. "It doesn't matter. Let's just try and get this meeting over and done with, shall we?"

He nodded, grateful that I wasn't about to have some sort of a meltdown in such a public place. The truth was, however, that I had forgotten how to feel anything at all. Apart from worry.

I was worried about how Teddy's death might catch up with me one day.

4

"Want to catch a flick after we've been in?"

Mike had cheered up considerably since his teary moment on the underground. It didn't surprise me, not in the slightest, as it seemed like everyone's duty to simply button up and keep going at the receipt of bad news.

"No, I don't think so, Mike. Not after what happened last time."

"Yeah, I suppose you're right. Sorry…Don't really know what comes over me when I'm in London. I love the hustle and bustle of it all."

"You get bored of it eventually," I muttered, as I longed for the peace and tranquillity of the Cornish countryside once again. I found myself dreaming of the sweetened raspberries that Mrs Philips had grown on her land, not entirely giving me the permission to pick them that I so craved. Nonetheless, more than a couple ended up perched on my tongue whenever I felt as though I was alone.

"I suppose we should get out of here as soon as we can," Mike carried on, shouting now to be heard over the toots of buses and a policeman's whistle. "Especially the way the Luftwaffe has been carrying on."

"I'd like that, Mike."

I tried to flood my mind with happier images than the ones that were slowly trying to creep back into my mind, the seeds of solemnity that I had been fighting so hard these past few weeks. But, as I had learned in time, once they had started, there was nothing that I could do to stop them.

Within a flash, I felt like I was stood back in the exact spot that I had been stood in, just over four weeks before. Everything looked the same to me, the wagons and trucks that trundled around as if there was no law keeping them restrained, the single police constable, white gloves and all, trying his best to hold back the onslaught of the revving engines. Mike was stood next to me.

"What do you say to a quick trip to the pictures?" he asked me, a mischievous grin just sliding into the corner of his mouth. He always did that. He always made a proposition that he knew I would hate, but knew that he would eventually drag me along. It was that little smile of his, it was captivating.

He never seemed to want to do anything without me, if I refused, he would simply not go to whatever it was he had suggested. A dance, a film, even a trip to the local bookshop, he would always require me as his chaperone to attend with him.

"It's getting a bit late, isn't it?" I asked, looking at my watch and immediately realising that it was a lot earlier than I had previously thought. Maybe I could have spent another hour or two with my family.

"It's only four, old boy. Plenty of time for a film. We'd be back at Weald in no time."

RAF North Weald had been the home of 249 Squadron for the past month or so, having previously been down in Wiltshire. Most of the lads seemed to hate it, being so close to London, yet being so far away. There seemed to be an invisible pull of the capital to those young men. Probably something to do with the alcohol, nightlife and the apparently plentiful supply of women.

But, for me, London symbolised something more than the short-lived thrills that the others pined for. For me, it was home. It was where I had grown up, and where I had intended to settle until *Herr Hitler* had stuck his jackboot in.

"Okay," I had conceded to Mike, "But only a film. We are not going to one of your little pubs."

"Understood, Red One," he said, with another wry smile accompanied by a wink.

I did not care too much for whatever it was we were about to watch, but Mike seemed sufficiently excited for the two of us. Instead, I became enthralled by the organ that was playing down at the front of the theatre, watching the little man's legs dance around just as much as his fingers, producing one mesmerising performance.

The little man with the short legs disappeared far too soon, and the curtains were drawn back, rather spectacularly, as the newsreel began to play.

As soon as we saw the subjects of the first segment, both Mike and I slumped further into our seats. We knew exactly what this would mean.

"Scramble! They're in the cockpits of their Spitfires and Hurricanes before you can say 'Bob's your Uncle!'

There's a job of work for these pilots and boy, do they love their work!"

"He's joking, right? Do you love your work, Johnny? No? Me neither. Who do they ask for these things?"

"Way up in the sky there are Messershmitts, Junkers, Heinkels or Dorniers, that are going to get the thrashing of their lives. Here they come Jerry, you rotten Swas-stinkers, you!"

The accompanying footage of Spitfires and Hurricanes scrambling to meet their enemies was indeed stirring stuff, which was exactly what two boys in uniform did not want right now. Especially as they wanted to make as quick a getaway as was possible. From previous experience, there was a chance that we would be mobbed by a group of young boys before we could leave, each one wanting a piece of German bomber, or maybe even an Iron Cross that we had somehow inexplicably found in our possession.

"I hate these things," I muttered under my breath, which was met with a grunt of recognition by Mike.

Neither of us wanted to be seen at that point in the day.

I did not pay much attention to the film, but I suddenly pulled myself to as gunshots began to ricochet all around me. It was only when I realised that I had dropped off, that the gunshots were merely a part of the film that I had been dragged to see.

Mike seemed to be thrilled with how everything was going.

Suddenly, and for a moment I found myself quite pleased with the Germans' sense of timing, the screen before us suddenly went to black, only to be replaced with a declaration that only required one to read the first line.

AN AIR RAID WARNING HAS JUST BEEN RECEIVED.

I looked across at Mike, he seemed incensed.

"Isn't that just typical of Jerry? They've been interrupting everything I've done for the last three months, and they can't even let me have a night off!"

I ignored him, instead opting to read the rest of the notice before us, which struggled to be seen over the groans and complaints offered up by everyone in the theatre.

The management suggest that you remain in the building but anyone desiring to leave is free to do so now.

No one seemed to be panicked or scared, just a general air of annoyance began to overcome everyone, as most of our congregation slowly made their way to the exits. No one was going to listen to the suggestion of the management, they had become too experienced in these raids to stay inside.

"Come on then, old boy," I grunted, slapping Mike on the back. "Another time maybe."

"Yes, yes. Alright. Another time."

Almost as soon as we had arisen from our seats, the unmistakeable sound of an air raid siren began to scream out into the night. I was quite shocked at how loud it seemed inside that cinema, but soon found myself pushing it to the back of my mind.

As a second siren started up, trying its hardest to catch up with the wails and falls of the first, I gripped Mike's wrist, spinning him round to face me.

"Cor!" he exclaimed, rubbing his shoulder as he turned. "You could have had my whole arm off there!"

"Reckon we could make it to the underground? We could still get back to Weald in time if we can."

"Worth a shot, I suppose," he grumbled back, still put out that I had nearly dislocated his shoulder.

By the time we had made it to the exit of the cinema, the ever-faithful anti-aircraft guns had already opened up, and it was not difficult to imagine the shouting and swearing that would be going on for the next few hours, as the men tried with earnest to keep up the constant barrage of shells.

The low, imposing boom would be followed, about twenty seconds later by a softer crump, in which time another two shells could already be on their way up to their targets. To the average

Londoner, the thought of shooting down one of the bombers was an exciting and achievable prospect, but to us flyboys, we knew that the chances of them hitting anything was rather slim. The best that they could hope for would be to knock one or two planes off their course.

It was a surprise to me that the last thing I should hear would be the bombers themselves. The complete onrush of noise seemed to confuse me no end, as I tried to make sense of the wails of the sirens, the sombre thuds of anti-aircraft guns and the harrowing howl of oncoming bombers.

There was a part of me that wanted a Hurricane to suddenly appear before me in the street, so that I could get up there and give them a welcoming blast of my eight Browning machine guns. As we stood there, gazing dozily towards the night sky, I knew that Mike was having exactly the same kind of thoughts.

"If only we could get up there. What do you say, Mike?"

"I reckon we could do more than those artillery boys ever could, Johnny."

There was a mesmerising element to it all, intoxicating almost. It was like having a beer or two and realising that you should stop, but you just couldn't. I was only worried about the fact that, by the time you had had another pint, it was always too late. I didn't want that to be the case with us two.

"Come on, Mike. We better get going!" I was now screaming at the top of my lungs, as the bombers began to drone directly overhead, no doubt releasing their payload that had both 'Johnny Parker' and 'Michael Hope' scratched into its casings.

We began to sprint the four hundred or so yards towards the nearest underground stop, where we intended to hop on the next service running east. From there we would hopefully be able to get onto an overground train back up to RAF North Weald. That was assuming the trains above the ground would still be running. Either way, we would be nearer to our destination.

It was only as we skidded around onto Great Windmill Street that we started to notice that the pitter-patter of our footsteps, splashing in a few puddles that had been left by the firefighters from a previous raid, was not the only noise that had joined us on the street.

Within seconds, the whole road seemed to be lit up in an eerie green light, so bright that I had to shield my eyes for a moment to adjust to it. They seemed to be littered all over the street, with one or two green monsters sliding their way down the tiles and slates of the rooftops all around us.

We both stopped in our tracks, once again mesmerised by it all.

"Cor!" exclaimed Mike for the second time in three minutes. "What are they?"

I walked towards one of the hissing tubes, that seemed no longer than fifteen inches long. It poured out an almost perfect white smoke, to accompany the brilliant green that it was producing, that I was sure the groundsman at Lords would have been proud of.

An air raid warden suddenly screamed around the corner, throwing small sheets of fabric on every single source of the green hiss that he could see, and putting an end to my own fun as he extinguished the one that lay just a few feet from me.

"What are they?" I called after him as he continued down the road.

"Incendiaries!" he screamed back. "Now get to a shelter!"

I looked back towards Mike, just as the sky behind his head seemed to light up in a fantastic streak of white light, as if someone had just switched all the lights back on again. A beam of light rose high into the sky, swaying and swishing, trying to catch anything in its gaze.

"So much for a blackout," I muttered to Mike as he reached me. "Come on, let's get down there sharpish."

It was as we picked up our pace again that the volume of AA shells that were tossed into the air increased dramatically. Things were about to get even louder around here.

Fortunately, we would be on the next tube out of West London.

5

"Johnny? Johnny? You okay?"

"Hmm? Oh, sorry. Yes, I am fine. I was just thinking about that night."

"Probably best that you don't do that mate."

"Yeah…"

It was a bit late to tell me that now, I thought, with an air of animosity towards him. It was a trait that I had long tried to get a hold of, but I could never stop myself fully silently berating the ones I loved for doing nothing more than trying to help me.

"Well then," he announced. "This is it."

I looked at the building before us. It was tired, small and altogether most underwhelming.

"Are you sure?" I asked him, having expected something much grander.

"Yep. Sixty-four Baker Street," he said, looking down at the small card in his hand. "This is most definitely it."

"It's hardly worth getting out of bed for."

"At least you had a bed to get out of," he muttered, with another cheeky grin to match. I knew what he had meant. The chaps in the squadron would have been sat in dispersal huts for most of the time that I had been away, with little chance to get some sleep apart from that which you could steal in an uncomfortable chair. Even that was fraught with unimaginable risk. Especially if one of the jokers in the squadron couldn't get any sleep themselves.

More than once, men of the squadron had been scrambled to meet bandits with a painted-on moustache that matched *Herr Hitler's* own. There was a hilarious irony attached to it somewhere. But for the life of me, I could not see it.

"Come on then, let's find out what was worth dragging you all the way from Cornwall for."

Although I did not want to admit to it just yet, the urgent message that was passed to me from the detective sergeant who came to see me at Mrs Philips' farmhouse had been a welcome one.

I had been there for three weeks, to rest and recuperate. But it was true that the last few days that I had spent there, I could feel myself going quite mad. I had nothing to do while I was there, no focus.

It is exceptionally testing for a young man to go from such a high-adrenaline day-to-day life like that on 249 squadron, to the polarised world of the Cornish countryside.

There were no signs of war there, which was what I had wanted, but it was so far removed from what had become my reality that I despised it. I wanted a reason to head back east. I needed to be back with the other boys, I missed them. All of them. I especially missed Teddy Higgins.

I tried to push the image of a small man tumbling helplessly from his cockpit, as he began his descent to earth. I sought to rid myself of the figure, as he began to flap around, not too dissimilar to a bird, as he attempted to pull the D-Ring of his parachute.

"It's not working!" he would have screamed to himself, as he began yanking at it, again and again, the ground rising to meet him at an alarming rate.

Tears began to rush to my eyes as I thought of Teddy, and wondered at what point the realisation would have set in, at what point had he given up?

If I knew him at all, then I could well imagine that his arm was still twitching around the D-Ring long after he had hit the ground. He was just that sort of chap.

"Flying Officers John Parker and Mike Hope. We were given these and told to come here as soon as possible."

"Ah right," muttered the young girl sat behind the desk. Mike looked over to me, a grin already on his face. I knew what that meant; he was in love.

She was pleasant enough looking, if a little serious, but I could not say that I found her particularly attractive. But, then again, I had hardly found anything attractive at all in the last few weeks. I was still finding it difficult to get back to normality. Whatever that was.

"Can I see your papers please?"

The girl began to inspect them, incredibly carefully and, for a moment or two, I became increasingly concerned that she was about to out me as an enemy spy.

"Major Hubbard is on the second floor. He will be with you shortly."

"Thanks awfully," said Mike, his strong, well-rounded tones on display far more than they normally were. They only ever seemed to become so overt when there was a lady present, a young, pretty one, in particular.

"I don't suppose," Mike started, as the girl handed us back our papers, "that you know of any good watering holes around here, do you?"

The girl looked up, not at all surprised at his question, perhaps ever so slightly irritated by the amount of times that she was asked.

"The Hertford Arms, Mayfair. They pull a good pint."

"Oh, jolly good. Far from here, is it?"

"About twenty minutes or so, I suppose."

I stood there awkwardly while the exchange continued, the girl looking over at me a number of times, as if she was expecting me to pull him off her. She knew what was coming.

"Excellent. Excellent. Maybe we could try that out after, Johnny? Hang on a minute, why don't you come with us? You'll be able to show us where it is."

The girl smiled politely, "No, thank you. I don't really mix well with your sort."

"Your sort…"

"Come on then, Mike," I interrupted, about thirty seconds too late, "let's go and see this Major, shall we?"

I smiled apologetically at the girl as I walked past, with the kind of face that said, "I really am so sorry about him."

With a slight smile in the corner of her mouth, her head bowed back down towards her desk, she continued rifling through the papers that she had been attending to earlier on.

"Your sort?" he repeated. "What did she mean by that?"

"Probably because you support West Ham, mate."

"Oh, don't remind me. I've been missing the football ever since it was suspended," he had a moment of contemplation, as he thought back to all the games that he had witnessed down at the Boleyn Ground.

"Oh, come on," I said, slapping him on the shoulder, "it can't be all that bad. At least they're not losing for one thing."

"I'm sure they would give it a jolly good go at it, if they had half the chance."

"What about the wartime league? You've got football there."

"Not the same," he muttered as we began to climb the stairs. "Standards are slipping all the time. Games called off. Not enough players to really call a team. That reminds me, I heard that Terry Woodgate joined up not that long ago. That's another of our regulars gone."

"I hope they all make it home."

"Me too. Come to think of it, I hope I make it home too," he chuckled softly as we climbed the stairs, getting to the second floor.

There was another girl, at another desk, not as pretty as the one before, but still pleasant enough. It seemed, though, that Mike had had his fingers well and truly burnt. He wasn't going to be trying again in this building. Especially when there was half a chance that none of them mixed with 'our sort.'

After words were exchanged with her, we were shown to a door. I had always imagined that majors and the like hid behind larger doors than the one we were presented with, far grander and more imposing than the dark oak, but otherwise rather plain door.

"Major Hubbard," announced the girl. "Flying Officers Hope and Parker, Sir."

"Ah, yes," breathed the Major, in the kind of throaty way that only a member of the upper class can do. "Gentlemen, please come in. Come in."

He clicked the lid of a pen back into its housing and stood up, as we both offered him a salute, which was only returned in the form of a handshake.

"Gents, I hope you don't mind my brevity, but I'd

rather like to get straight to the point of this meeting. I have quite a few people that I am due to see over the next few hours. Please, take a seat."

We perched ourselves on the green leather chairs that awaited us on the opposite side of the desk to the Major.

"Hope and Parker. Hope and Parker," he muttered to himself, a couple of times, before sliding two files from the mountain that he had stockpiled on his desk. There were so many there, the tower slowly teetering to one side, that I anticipated he had half the files that the British military kept on its personnel.

He clicked his tongue a few times as he perused our files, reminding himself of our service record and whatever else might be stored in one of those things. I had never had the fortune to look inside one.

Mike and I both sat stony-faced, arms on laps and ready for a dressing down in front of the headmaster. He had seemed friendly enough as we had been welcomed in, but even the nicest of men could turn into the ugliest at the drop of a hat.

"Michael Hope."

"Yes, Sir."

"Born 1917. Educated at St John's College Cambridge, studying history, art and architecture. Represented your college in rugby, cricket and football. You're quite the sportsman," remarked the Major, switching the files in front of him, presumably to my own.

"Flying Officer John Parker. Also born in 1917.

Also educated at St John's studying English and French Literature. You too represented St John's in cricket and football. Did you not fancy playing ruggers?"

"Not quite my scene, Sir."

"Fair enough. Of course, I am an Oxford man myself. But I won't hold that against you. From what I have heard you two have an exemplary record. Quite the fliers so I'm told."

"Thank you, Sir."

He shuffled around, drawing a pipe from under all the rubble of his desk. He stood up for a moment, to get a bird's eye view of the worktop, before catching sight of his target.

He shook the little box of matches around in front of us, "There they are."

He took his time lighting it, before turning to the two, very confused men who sat before him.

"Now I suppose you're both wondering why you are here. There's nothing to worry about, I can assure you. I just wanted to ask you a few questions. I hope that is okay with you?"

He angled his speech upwards, as if it was a genuine question, but we had both been around these types of men before, and knew full well that his question was, in actual fact, a statement.

It would have been far more pertinent to have said, "I am going to ask you a few questions. Whether you like it or not."

The Major walked to the window located behind his desk, which allowed both Mike and I to exchange a confused look with one another.

"Now, Parker. Judging by the fact that you are studying French literature, am I right in presuming that you can speak French?"

"Yes, Sir."

"How good are you?"

"I spent many summers over there, Sir. When I was a youngster."

"*Alors, es-tu bon?*" he asked, turning to me.

"Yes, Sir. I'd like to think that I am rather good."

He broke out into a wry smile, one that seemed to tell me that he had found exactly what it was that he had been looking for. I was not entirely sure if being one of his chosen ones was a matter for elation or a cause for concern.

"Any other languages?"

"A bit of German, Sir. Enough to get by."

"And you, Hope. You are something of an artist, I gather. You spent time in France recently, I believe."

"Yes, Sir. In Paris. At the *École nationale supérieure des Beaux-Arts* school."

"Never heard of it myself…But then again, my drawing is no better than a child's. How long were you there?"

"Six months, Sir."

"Good. Good."

We had been in the office for about a quarter of

an hour now, and although we had been there on the promise of brevity, we were still no clearer as to our purpose for being there.

"Sir, what's this all about?"

"We are looking for good chaps like you. Who have spent time in France recently and understand the culture. Translation work mainly. You'll find out more soon enough. I'd like you to report to one of our preliminary schools in Sussex. June will give you all the details on your way out."

"*Our* schools, Sir?" Mike enquired, as the same thought had rushed to my mind at the word choice.

"Yes. All will be revealed to you in good time gents. As I said, you have nothing to worry about. Right then, off you go. Don't forget to see June."

We got up to leave, saluting the man who already had started to brief himself on the next visitors that he would perplex.

"Oh, just one other thing," the Major piped up as we reached the door. "What were you doing in Cornwall, Parker?"

"I was resting, Sir."

"In a funk hole?"

"That was not my purpose for being there, Sir. I was trying to adapt to how my life would be now."

"Yes, I read about that in your file. A tragedy. I'm most terribly sorry—"

"It does not matter now, Sir. It is done. Nothing I can do about it now."

We left the room without so much of another word, but I had been ruffled by his closing comments to me. I really did hate it when people kept trying to bring that situation back into my mind, especially after I had tried so hard to forget it.

6

As I walked through the creaking doors of the Hertford Arms, I couldn't help but wonder if Mike had had another go at trying to chat up the young woman who had recommended the pub to us in the first place.

I quickly ran my eyes over the pub, which didn't take me too long, as it was only a small one, not the kind of pub that I was used to frequenting at all. The bar rang the length of the establishment, curving into an oval at the edges to lead to some back rooms. Around the perimeter was a mixture of old, stained-glass adorned booths and some rickety looking tables, the kind that looked far too unsteady to trust a pint on top of it.

But Mike, the kind of chap that would trust Herr Hitler with his grandmother's life, was sat in the corner patiently, two pints wobbling precariously on the tabletop.

"Hello Johnny. Over here, I've got one in for you already!"

He was sat in all his finery, as Flying Officer Hope and, all in all, he looked quite dashing as he sat quietly in the pub, all alone. But there wasn't a single woman around to take him in, not even a schoolboy ready and waiting to be regaled by his daring adventures in the sky. The whole place, save one stool that occupied a haggard old man, was barren.

"Was that girl having us on when she recommended this place?"

He chuckled slyly, as we both lifted our pints to our lips in unison, as I was frightfully nervous that an imbalance on one side of the table would send the whole thing sloshing into my lap.

"Not sure, really. But we'll find out soon enough. I'm meeting her here later on."

I looked up at him, the darkened features of his face suddenly illuminated in jubilation and triumph.

"You managed to wear the poor thing down then?"

"Oh yes," he replied, "I always do, don't I?"

He did, somehow. He was never particularly confident, there was some sort of deep-seated discomfort that rumbled in the pit of his stomach, but as soon as he was around a woman, especially a pretty one, everything seemed to ebb away.

I supposed that it had something to do with his own looks, not handsome in the conventional sense but handsome enough. His dark wavy hair, which was slicked back with enough Brylcreem to drown a whale, revealed a small forehead, which seemed almost inadequate for the size of his head.

His eyes were set back and dark, his face a maze of shadows and crevices. Everything, upon first glance, would hint at a deadly serious man, one of such severity that you daren't look at him for too long, in case he captured your soul. But in actuality, that couldn't have been further from the truth, which is why he caught the attention of so many women.

The way that his darkened face would suddenly explode into a wide-eyed and toothy grin was enough to perplex anyone and, if he held their attention for long enough, they would be trapped.

"So, come on then. What did Hubbard want with you this time?"

I took another sip of the warm beer in front of me, still far nicer than anything I tried down at Telwyn farm, as I mulled over the second appointment that I had with Major Hubbard, the man who had mysteriously summoned us just over a week before.

I tried to formulate something for him but, for the life of me, I could not think about what had happened.

Hubbard had hardly revealed anything to me whatsoever as to what our involvement in his little project might have been, but instead simply chatted to me, about my life, about my time in Hurricanes and my family.

"Still not quite sure, Mike. He asked me the same old questions. This time with a lot more French involved. He tried me in Italian and German as well."

"Didn't know you dabbled in those languages too, old fruit."

"I don't. Not really anyway. Enough to ask for a coffee and the way to the train station, but that's about it."

"That's more than me anyway."

"I think interpretive work is where we're headed, you know."

Mike disagreed as he mustered a grunting noise as he took an over-exuberant sip from his glass. It took one painful swallow before he could explain himself.

"If it was interpretive work," he mumbled, lowering his voice so that the haggard man at the bar couldn't hear a single syllable, "then why was he asking me so much about my art school?"

"Oh?"

"Yeah. He asked me to draw what I could remember of the school. The grounds, the rooms, anything that I could recall of it. Wanted me to draw it all from memory."

"But you were there years ago."

"Exactly. And the place is bigger than Buckingham Palace. I'm certain of it. I was only there for a short while. Not exactly long enough to learn the blueprints of the place."

"So, how did it go?"

He pulled a face that told me he thought he had done far better than he was expecting.

"A few rooms were probably out of proportion. But all in all, a damn fine effort."

We sat in silence for a few minutes, staring towards the bottom of our glasses and wishing that we were somewhere else. For me, it was back with all the others at 249 Squadron, who I had not seen in some time now. For Mike, I was certain that it was back at the front desk of Major Hubbard's office, chatting to the young woman that he would shortly be meeting.

After what felt like an eternity of deafening silence, Mike spoke.

"I dreamt about Teddy Higgins last night. Actually, every night really. Since it happened."

Instinctively, I rolled my neck around, a satisfying pop happening just after a half-roll. It was something that had plagued me for many months now, a result of constantly checking all around the skies for that faint black dot that we were aiming to intercept.

Now, all it did was cause me pain, that needed to be relieved every now and then, my chosen times to do so frequently being when I felt grotesquely uncomfortable or wary.

"You shouldn't dwell on it so much. These things have a habit of lingering around. They make you question what you could have done."

"I'm sure I could have done something."

"Like what, Mike? You were fifteen thousand feet in the air. You could hardly hop out and catch him."

"I know. I know. But I could have stopped him from getting hit like that."

"Mike, listen to me. This is a war we're in. People have died and will continue to do so. In all likelihood we'll snuff it soon enough. Do you reckon the other lads will dwell on you so much?"

"I'd like to think so."

"They have a job to do, Mike. It's only because you're off ops at the moment that is making you think like this."

It hurt me to talk to him in such a forceful manner, but it was exactly what I needed to hear myself. No one would linger on my own demise for a moment longer than they needed to. They would have a beer in my name and be back up in the skies the very next day. That was just how it went in this war.

But every now and then, someone stuck in your mind. Someone lingered for an hour or two longer than they should have done. But it was those that would have you spiralling out of control at fifteen thousand feet, with hot oil bubbling out all over you. They were the ones that could make you lose your focus.

"Want another?" I nodded my head towards his empty glass, before swiping it up in my grasp and getting it refilled.

As I headed back towards the table, I caught sight of the young lady that had greeted us on our arrival at Major Hubbard's offices. I was both surprised and pleased to see her there, standing on the other side of the street, waiting for a bus to pass by before skipping across the road. I hated the thought of Mike sitting in the pub on his own, waiting for his date that would never arrive.

I plonked the drinks down on the table, rather too hard as the legs began rattling on the uneven floor.

"I better drink mine nice and quick."

"Why's that?"

"Your girl is here, that's why."

"Aren't you staying?"

"You're pulling my leg, aren't you? Why on earth would I want to stay? I find it uncomfortable enough just watching you talk to them, never mind sharing a drink too."

"Fair enough."

I took a large sip from my glass, without sitting down, as I watched the girl daintily make her way towards the doors of the Hertford Arms.

"Here, you take the rest."

"What? No, she'll think I'm addicted to the stuff."

"Just tell her you're thirsty. Good luck, Mike."

As I spun on my heel, I suddenly remembered one of the questions that had been burning a hole in my mind for the whole journey to the pub, but it was one that I had completely neglected in my conversation with Mike.

I glanced at the girl, whose arm was now slightly outstretched and reaching for the door. For a brief moment, I thought about abandoning the question altogether, in case she was to report back to Major Hubbard that we had broken his rule of silence.

"Mike," I gasped as I dashed back to the table, sloshing some of his two pints over the surface. "Do you know any Morse code?"

"I did a signals course some years ago. When my father wanted me in the Navy. But it was a long time ago now. Then of course when I did flight training, but I wasn't great at it. Why's that?"

"Just something our friend said to me earlier on. Thought that it was a bit strange."

His face looked puzzled for a moment before he locked eyes with his new accomplice, at which point his darkened face began to shine like a beacon.

"Hello."

"Sorry, I was just leaving."

"Oh, please don't leave on my account, Flying Officer Parker."

"It's alright. I have other places to be. And please, it's Johnny."

I spun away for a second time, pulling my cap on over my darkening, ruffled hair, just before I got to the door.

I glanced over at Mike for one final time, already working his inexplicable magic over the young girl, with a look that said, 'We'll talk later.'

We would have plenty to talk about, especially as my little mind began to whir and creak as I tried my hardest to think about what it was Hubbard wanted us to do.

We would both see him again in the next week or so, for yet another interview that would for some reason be conducted in an amalgamation of English, French, German and Italian. No doubt he would probe into more of our seemingly unconnected talents; art, sporting prowess and the ability to make snap decisions.

The more thought I gave it, as I skulked around the streets of London, waiting for Mike to finish his rendezvous, the more it began to terrify me.

There had never been an option for me to refuse a meeting with this Major, and it didn't seem like there would be a way out at all.

For the first time since leaving Telwyn Farm, I thought about returning there. Under a different name, with a different story altogether. There would be no fooling Mrs Philips, but she seemed like the kind of lady that would turn a blind eye for a pound or two.

I needed to get away. I needed to leave this war behind and everything that it was asking me to do and everything that it had already taken from me. I was in desperate need of a new life altogether.

7

There was a very faint drizzle just beginning to slowly slide its way down from the heavens, making a marvellous job at dampening my clothes, but more so my spirits. I felt like doing the only thing that I knew how to in this sort of situation to buoy myself, and that was to look across at Mike.

He could sense my apprehension, he knew me well enough to be able to read the slightest change in my face, and as ever, he tried his hardest to distract me from the fear of failure that I had become so accustomed to.

"We're making good progress, old fruit."

"I wish you wouldn't call me that."

"Why not?"

"I don't know. But it makes me sound like something you would find at the bottom of a forgotten garden."

Mike thought for a moment, clearly debating

whether or not the thought that had come into his mind would be an appropriate one to voice. It was unusual, for him to consider what it was that he was about to say, for he had often dived headfirst into hot water, on account of his eager tongue.

Nevertheless, he decided it was worth the risk.

"I suppose Telwyn farm could be considered something of a forgotten garden."

I looked at him, as we progressed down the country lane, adorned either side by nettles and decaying berries, the misty-like rain more kissing my cheek than hitting it. The clean water, its chill and simplicity, reminded me no end of Telwyn farm, and of the little stream that I had frequented, fully clothed.

For a fleeting moment, I was perplexed that he had known the name of the establishment that I had spent almost a month of my life staying at. But quickly, it turned to annoyance and frustration, that he had somehow gone rifling behind my back, without having the decency to have asked me to my face.

"Why would you say something like that?" I asked, with a tone of anger that was hardly an accident.

"I just thought that, maybe, you needed to talk about it all."

"There's nothing for me to talk about, Mike."

"Oh, come off it Johnny. You need to at some point. You can't just forget it forever. Besides, we'll be leaving soon, and I don't want slip-ups from you."

"What makes you think there will be any?"

He looked to the ground for a while, our footsteps crunching on the sodden gravel as the rainfall really began to find its strength.

I knew as well as he did that I was a walking liability and, some days I wasn't even a walking one. More of a stumble. He was right, I knew that I had to get it all off my chest eventually, but for some inexplicable reason, I simply desired nothing more than to hide it all away under lock and key, and pretend that nothing had ever happened.

This was my chance at a completely new life. One where no one would know my real name, or my background, what troubled or concerned me. It was a chance to start afresh, without the constant worrying glances or pitying apologies.

"It wasn't your fault, you know. You shouldn't blame yourself. You're a decent fellow and you have every—"

"Be quiet."

"Oh, come on. I'm trying to big you up here. Most chaps would take a pew and lap it all up."

"No. Shut up. Use your eyes for once. *Regardez.*"

For once in his life, he did as he was told. I supposed that it was because it was most unusual for me to command such attention in the way that I had done, or the downright shock at my impertinence.

But as he listened to my instruction, his head

began to turn, slowly, so that he did not give off an impression of being surprised or nervous. He did not do so with any particular kind of emotion, he just looked.

Dead ahead of us, walking with a slight limp but still managing to hold his body in a taught, proud posture, was a member of the *Gendarmerie*. The arrogance with which the man seemed to walk, was only accentuated by the uniform that he had pulled over him, the immaculate creases and glistening buttons adding a certain sparkle to the man's eyes.

His kepi hat, complete with a thin white band around the top, was on at an odd angle, as if the peak was pointing to one or two o'clock, rather than the customary twelve.

It was a uniform that I had been used to seeing for many weeks now, having studied photographs and drawings of every variation imaginable, from what might be worn on a hot summer's day, to the all the more sombre affair that was adorned on a dingy, misty December's evening.

"What should we do?" he asked, looking up to me as a schoolboy to his father. I resisted the temptation to look down on him, as I knew that his face, with features so sunken that he always looked as if he was in a darkened room, would be glaring back at me with the hope of a small puppy.

"What do you mean? What else can we do?"

He thought about my question for a second or two, as we both naturally slowed our pace to avoid the inevitable meeting with the *Gendarme*. It was something that we had been taught to do, to give ourselves a little longer to run through our stories, or to give the officer a chance to deviate in his path and move on elsewhere.

"We could always turn around, Johnny. Make out as if we've forgotten something and head home."

"Mike, we'd have half the German army on top of us before we could even take a step. It's too late now. Make sure you know your story."

"But..." his voice trailed off until there was no other sound but the trickling of the mist on the trees that flanked us, and the crunch of the gravel that ground and rolled under the weight of our feet.

Ever since we had started our training, I had realised that Mike was the kind of chap that wanted out of every situation that he felt cornered in. It was strange, for a pilot who had shot down at least four and a half enemy aircraft. Just a half away from becoming a fighter ace. I did not quite know what had caused him to become predisposed to such a stance, but there was a deep-seated unbelief in himself, a lack of confidence to such a scale that I considered even myself to be bolder in my own abilities.

I locked eyes with the *Gendarme* officer who was now only yards away from being within spitting distance from us. His eyes seemed to droop downwards at either end, like a pair of bananas, as if they had suffered some sort of crushing disappointment in his life that could never be remedied. Something like the occupation of the land that he had served for many years.

He was old, older than Mike and I put together, which could still put him under the age of fifty years old. But, despite that, his face told of a life hindered by pain and disappointment, but a life that he was keen to spend inflicting the same kind of misery on all those that he came across.

A faint smirk seemed to creep up one side of his face, as if the left-hand side was non-compliant in the game that he was playing.

"*Salut,*" he called out to us, perhaps a little too far away for the range of his voice. He repeated his salutation to us, this time a lot closer, so close in fact that we could both smell that he had only recently consumed his evening meal.

We replied, dutifully, maintaining a bold eye contact with the man, so as not to arouse any kind of suspicion that we were riddled with nerves. The truth was though, that we were, I was anyway. I was frightfully aware that at any moment he could blow down hard on his whistle and have us arrested. We would be in a police cell with interrogators all around us before we even had the chance to blink.

My palms had been clammy ever since we had been handed our objectives, but subconsciously I curled them up into fists as we stood there, in case the ample supply of perspiration began to roll off the tips of my fingers and drip on the gravelly ground.

My heart, rhythmically striking at the inside of my

skin, felt like it would give the whole game away and I began listening to it closely, petrified that it may have been banging out some sort of message in Morse.

A foolish supposition, but not one that was totally inconceivable to the paranoid state of mind that I had learned to live with.

My mind had been tuned in the last few weeks and months, rewired completely in some regards, to be suspicious of everything and everyone. The way that someone spoke would include indicators as to their real intentions, the manner in which a tree swayed would be determined by either a breeze or a movement behind it. I had been taught to never take things as I saw them. There was always something hiding behind everything.

"*Cartes d'identité.*"

We complied, removing the thick cards from our pockets before handing them to the *Gendarme's* outstretched palm.

As he inspected them, I inspected him. His dreary face made drearier still by the miserable rainfall, sloped down towards the ground, as if he wanted nothing more than to slump into a heap on the floor.

We had been taught to be careful around these men. Some, the most patriotic of Frenchmen, would stop at nothing to help us achieve our aims. Others, those with pockets being lined by the Germans, would do everything within their power to make sure that we were arrested and interrogated.

There was no way of distinguishing what side this chap was on.

I glanced to one side, as the man continued to rub his thumb over parts of the card, apparently testing to see how well made the card was and if any of the ink would rub off in the rain.

Mike was stood to my side, his eyes slowly filling up with water, as they always did when he was beginning to let his nerves overcome him. Other than me, I did not think that anyone else knew of this disposition and so, as long as he kept everything else in check, we would be okay.

"What are you gentlemen doing here, at this time of the evening?" the *Gendarme* queried, without really looking up from his inspection.

I felt the dryness of my own mouth, and assumed that the arid desert would be reproduced ten times over in Mike's own mouth, as it so often did.

"Well, officer…"

"We are just out enjoying this lovely weather."

I held back from glaring at Mike, instead, frozen to the spot, I watched the permanent smirk on the *Gendarme's* face begin to morph into something all the more sinister.

At first, it was a leer, the kind that screamed that we had just landed ourselves in the hottest kind of water known to man. But then it developed into something else, something far more comforting and satisfying.

He began to smile.

It was an expression that seemed foreign to the rest of his face, as if he hadn't known what a grin was since the days of his youth, which were long since passed. But the teeth were bared more and more, till the point where his mouth would stretch no further.

He passed our cards back to us, removed his kepi and ran his fingers through his hair.

"Very well done, chaps," he began as the cap was tucked under his arm. "You composed yourselves with a confidence that was both satisfactory and yet not exuberant."

The smile began to wane from his face, the upturned bananas returning to his eyes, and the altogether wearisome features returning to what they had been for the last few weeks.

"But do not ever interrupt one another again. It undermines one another. It makes it seem like you are hiding something, which simply cannot be apparent to an inspecting officer."

I felt the redness of Mike's skin worsen as the shame was heaped upon him by the bucket load.

"Remember gents, you are actors, in the largest play imaginable. A play in which the curtain will not be drawn for a good many months, possibly years. And if your audience is not convinced by your performance, you will be killed. It is as simple as that."

We both stood in front of our instructor, Captain Gallagher, dumbfounded at what he had said.

"You are to be Circuit Fortunae, is that correct?"

"Yes, Sir."

"Fortuna was the Roman god of good luck. Let's hope it stays on your side chaps."

We were mere weeks away from being in the field for real, but were still making mistakes, potentially fatal ones.

Mike and I would need to improve drastically in a short amount of time, otherwise, that curtain could be coming down on our lives much quicker than we would have liked.

8

It was not the first time that I had been in one of the Whitley bombers that Mike and I found ourselves in, but it was the first time that we were in one in the dead of night. The stillness of the night, the peace and serenity that I had so often enjoyed, was shattered by the two huge engines that roared on either side of the fuselage that we were both perched in.

It wasn't the most uncomfortable place to be, but there were certainly other places that I would have chosen to take a seat that wasn't in the belly of the aircraft. But still, it felt good to finally be back up in the air.

Months had passed since I had last been cruising around the skies at this kind of altitude and, although the speed was considerably less, I was still drawing an immense kick of finally being back in the sky.

What I was not enjoying however, was the fact that I was no longer in control, I wasn't the one in the cockpit enjoying a spectacular view of the British countryside as we glided around.

That was what I had missed the most about being in the Hurricane, the way in which I felt completely in control of my own destiny, and not even the sight of an enemy fighter would be able to sway me in that regard.

I felt superior to everyone and everything when I was up in the air, the second that the nose lifted, and the undercarriage was retracted. There was nothing between my backside and the ground, other than a light wooden structure, covered by a thin canvas.

It was that same thin canvas though, that would cause me all sorts of problems if I ever had an encounter with the enemy, their bullets being more than capable of zipping through one side and straight out the other, leaving two gaping wounds in what could only be described as my best friend.

"Hello Ganer leader. This is Cowslip control. Your customers are now over Gravesend. Vector zero-eight-zero. Angels two-zero."

It was all I could hear repeated through my mind as I sat in the back of the Whitley, reliving the days gone by where I was at the top of my game, flying side by side with my squadron as we hunted down the enemy.

No sooner had I thought about the rampaging success that we had achieved in shooting down hordes of enemy bombers, I had already begun to reminisce about the equally numerous disasters that we had been subjected to.

"Break! Break!" began to echo around my ears, as I fumbled between my legs to find the spade-like control that I would need to push forward into a dive. I would lose altitude as quickly as I could, to get out of the way of all the other planes now carving their way through the skies.

I would roll and bank, snapping my neck this way and that so as to check that I had nothing on my tail. Even when I was certain that there was no one around, I still remained as vigilant as ever.

The minute you thought you were comfortable, would be the time that you found yourself ditching in the English Channel.

As I pulled back on the imaginary control stick in between my legs, I pictured the lone 109 that was flying dead ahead of me. I thought for a moment that I was seeing things, as the aircraft was flying steadily southwards and hardly altering their course. Either the pilot inside was already dead or was silently wishing that he was.

With a slight adjustment to the throttle and a dabble with the mixture, I was soon directly behind the 109, still flying as straight as an arrow, with my Hurricane just below him.

I bided my time, every five or six seconds checking my own tail, in case it was all a part of a trap, to get me to fly as straight as him. But I could see nothing.

This pilot seemed like he was heading home after a training sortie, not flying over his enemy's territory.

Gently, with the slightest of jolts, I pulled back on the spade with my right hand, gripping it tightly, the sweat beginning to seep into the lining of my gloves. With my left hand, perspiring with an equal effort, I pushed the throttle forwards gently, so that I could rise up and match the altitude of the 109.

His tail was now perfectly in my gunsight and I quickly had to correct myself before I flew higher than him. Even if I was just an inch too high, he would see me, and no doubt be out of my grasp in no time.

Holding the whole aircraft as steady as I could, my thumb moved to cover the button that would activate my weaponry.

I closed my eyes gently, just letting in enough sunlight to constantly remind myself that I was still awake, as I said a quick prayer for the man who would soon be going down. It wasn't a confidence reason that I did it, but out of a genuine respect and care for the man inside. I was firing to shoot down his aircraft, not to kill the poor soul inside. I always hoped that the Luftwaffe pilots that we came across shared the same mentality.

Opening my eyes fully, every sense suddenly ran away from me, as my only focus became the eight .303 machine guns that flanked me in my cockpit. The rattling that filled my ears rumbled its way through my core, shaking at my ears so much that I thought they would begin to bleed.

The sky that had, until recently, been a picture of blue and peacefulness, was now full of glowing fury, as the tracer rounds made their way to the aircraft.

I watched as sparks began to fly as some rounds bounced off the wings of the 109, others penetrating the surface and burrowing their way into the fuselage.

All of a sudden, I found myself flying straight into a cloud of black, at which point my thumb shot back from the trigger and I throttled back.

One of my rounds must have got extremely lucky, somehow finding its way into the fuel tank that sat just behind the cockpit. A great stream of black, like a pot of paint was spilling from underneath, had begun billowing out of the 109.

Instinctively, I climbed, to get out of the way of what could soon be an airworthy fireball. The 109 too, climbed, but banked hard to the right as the pilot inverted his aircraft. There was no hope for him to get home, he knew that he would be bailing out.

I watched and began chanting to myself as he went through the motions of trying to get out.

"Bail out, you fool! Bail out!"

As the billowing black turned to an orange, the man still refused to fall from his aircraft, the hinged cockpit canopy staying well and truly closed.

I continued my warning to the man as I circled over the area of his stricken aircraft, as it rapidly dropped towards the sea, but still he refused to listen.

I wondered for a moment if the man was already dead, or possibly overcome by the fumes that would now be engulfing his cockpit. But, finally, I saw the hatch limply fall open, right about the same time that the whole thing exploded into a huge fireball.

I scanned the area for a few more seconds, holding a circling pattern directly above where the aircraft had been. But there was nothing. There was no parachute opening that I was praying for and, several seconds after the explosion, I resigned myself to the fact that there never would be one.

It was only as I levelled out, that I realised my grave error. At first, I only heard the sound of the air being displaced over the tops of my wings, but then I saw—

"Everything alright, old fruit? You look somewhat distracted."

As the Whitley bomber continued to drone and wobble around the air, I suddenly realised that it was all over. I was no longer in Hurricanes. I would no longer be nose-to-tail with the enemy and ducking and diving to avoid 109 machine gun rounds.

I was now in the Whitley, preparing to fall through the aperture in the belly of the aircraft, which was far more testing than it had first sounded.

"You jump through that hole there," the instructor had said, pointing to the gap that had opened up in front of him. "When you go through, make sure you go through the centre of the hole. Keep your body rigid and straight. Whatever you do, do not look down through the hole as you jump. Is that understood?"

"Why not, Sergeant?" Mike had asked. He was the only one who had the confidence to do so.

"Because, if you look down, you bend your body out of shape. And if you do that, there's a jolly good chance that your nose will be ringing the bell."

He smirked, which quickly returned to normal as he looked at the puzzled faces all around him.

"Ringing the bell means smacking your lovely little hooters on the inside of the aperture. There will be blood and they will be broken."

"Why ringing the bell?"

"You should hear the noise it makes. Plus," he added with a satisfying giggle in the back of his throat, "whoever rings the bell must buy everyone a drink down the pub. Everyone happy with that?"

Not everyone was, especially when having to fork out for twenty drinks, as well as nursing a very badly swollen nose.

It was a fate that I had, until now, avoided completely, but then again, the jumps that I had completed were in broad daylight, where it was easy to see the aperture.

"I'm fine," I shouted back to Mike over the din of the bellowing engines. "I'm just not sure I have enough money to be ringing the bell."

He chuckled back and leant into me, "Don't worry. If you do it, I won't tell any of the Frenchies on the ground. They'll be none the wiser."

He tapped the outside of his nose with his index finger, the international code for keeping a secret, but also a subtle reminder of what might happen if I was to misjudge my jump a little.

We sat in silence for the next half an hour, both of us mulling over what we had done with our lives so far, and what our task would be once we were on the ground.

For me, it was a minefield fraught with tragedy and triumph, which I quickly tried to ignore and instead thought about what might lie ahead.

"Right then, killer boys," screamed the jump-master as he waddled his way towards us. It was a name that the whole crew had assigned to us, instead of getting to know our actual names. Apparently, we weren't exactly flavour of the month with our Bomber Command counterparts. They weren't even interested in the fact that we had been the ones who had escorted their flights, multiple times.

"I'll open the hatch now. You know the drill. You won't be able to hear me when I do. But keep your eyes on me and watch for the signal."

We both gave him a thumbs up, as he replaced his mask over his face. Slowly, carefully, trying not to fall out himself, the hinge doors were opened, accentuating the tremendous noise of the engines on either side of us.

As he stepped back, I swung myself around, so that my feet were dangling out of the aircraft, leaning back so as not to get sucked out into the night just yet.

I kept my eyes on the jumpmaster, as I watched his mask flutter and flick around as he presumably spoke to the rest of his crew about the killer boys.

As I sat there, half in the bomber, half out, I couldn't help but think of what the people on the ground would be thinking.

Did they think that another bombing raid was on its way? Would they all be cowering in their shelters like I had been forced to do myself? Did they despise the crew members that were trying to liberate their country?

Everything was zipping through my mind as quickly as the thumb was thrust up into my face. Shuffling forwards, like the payload that was normally carried by this aircraft, I tumbled out, into the night.

9

I couldn't help but think of it as the mightiest thunderstorm that I had endured in my entire life. Every roll of thunder was tremendous, enthralling even, and the longer that I stood under its falling might, the longer I wanted to be in amongst the encounter.

As a child, I had been petrified of thunder, the way in which the universe seemed to flex its muscles and display how vicious it could be. My legs, nothing more than a pair of matchsticks back then, would quiver and tremble, until I would be forced to sit down, invariably under the dining room table with my mother.

"Get him out from there," my father would grumble, pipe in hand, chair facing the window. "He will have to learn to deal with it. Can't have a Parker scared of the weather. How utterly ridiculous."

"Leave him be, Walter. He's just a boy," my mother, a more compassionate soul than my father, was permanently stationed in my corner, ready to defend me.

"Bah," my father would mutter, as another clap of thunder rolled around the skies. His face, illuminated by the lightning that followed, would always brighten somehow in the darkness, as if each peal of thunder, displaying the untamed power of the skies, made him happier within.

My father, although expressed dispassionately, had been right, I did have to learn how to deal with it. As I became a more experienced pilot, it would be my duty to fly in adverse weather, to carry out patrols or to test radio equipment.

But then, I was able to deal with it in the most menial of ways. I would fly high, I would tickle the throttle and climb as high as I needed until the clouds, which buffeted at my wingtips and threatened to throw me from the skies, broke and I was in a comparative heavenly realm of brilliant blue.

As I stood at the foot of the pile of bricks that had once been someone's home however, I knew that there was no way for me to cope with this kind of thunderstorm. There was no break in the clouds for me to dive through, no dining room table for me to hide under. This was one thunderstorm that I simply could not ignore.

I looked up to the sky, an ominous blue colour, as if someone had left a lamp on in the corner of the heavens, as the fires that had started continued to make ground, against the best efforts of the firemen all around me.

I wiped away at an oily bead of sweat that had started to dribble from my forehead and found it to be an inky black colour. Immediately, I withdrew my handkerchief and began dabbing away at my face, trying in earnest to deny what was going on around me and find some sort of normality.

"Johnny, we should go. We are of no use here. CO will have our heads if we're much later."

I looked up at Mike and, for the first time, I sensed the genuine fear and alarm that was coursing through his body. He was experiencing this war with no weapons, with nothing that he could use to fight back, and he was alarmed.

"You go, Mike. I'm going to stay put."

"And do what?!" he blurted. "Stand there staring at the sky? Come on, let's go, now."

My gaze returned to the sky; its odd bluey hue still painted across the heavens. As I stared, my eyes became aware of the searchlights, great pillars of white, against an otherwise dull London sky.

They swept and scanned the skies, crossing one another from time to time in a friendly greeting. I locked on to one such beam, as it bowed westwards, only for it to stop momentarily and backtrack across the sky. From there, it moved more slowly, carefully sweeping the sky now and not in the carefree way it had seemed to before.

I tried to imagine the excitement of the young

lads who were operating the searchlight, frantically trying to keep the aircraft in their sights so that a nearby ack-ack gun could have a pop at sending one of them down.

I could have sworn that, over the orchestral volume of noise, I could hear the much older officers, some of whom had fought in the last war, telling them to be quiet and stay focused.

The belly of the doomed aircraft was flashing a brilliant white, as if the light bouncing off it had magnified its strength ten-fold. I watched as it was sent into a left-hand bank and right, and then finally a corkscrew manoeuvre to try and break out from the iron grip of the searchlight.

I couldn't imagine it was particularly fun for the crew inside, who I suddenly had an immense sympathy for, especially the navigator, whose timings and plottings would have been thrown completely out of the window.

I felt strange, as I felt, rather than saw, the ack-ack guns begin to open up, as a feeling began to surge around my body that I never thought possible. I wanted them to survive.

I felt like calling out 'Come on! You can do it!' but instead was rooted to the spot upon which I stood, with nothing coming from my mouth other than the rancid warmness of my breath as I excitedly watched.

Great balls of fury began to explode on either side of the aircraft, as it began to level out, apparently resigned to the fact that they might never be out of the searchlight's beam. Orange balls began to erupt closer and closer to the aircraft, until there was an ear-splitting bang, accompanied by an even larger sphere of fire, as one of the ack-ack rounds finally hit home.

"Johnny, come on!"

I watched as the inferno that broke out on the starboard wing of the bomber began to light the sky far better than the searchlight ever could.

Slowly at first, the bomber began to lose height, the searchlight still following its demise despite the three hundred other targets that were now roaring overhead. Over time though, it fell into a steep dive, as I imagined the pilot losing control over the beast and giving the order to bail out. That was if they were even still alive.

Within seconds, an orange explosion, as if the sun had risen doubly fast, glowed on the horizon, as the muffled thump reached my ears.

I stared for a few seconds more, as the searchlight went back to work to pick out another victim.

"Go," I muttered, quietly at first, before realising that the noise around me had drowned me out. "Go, Mike. I'm going to stay here. I can still help."

His shadowy and moody face stared back at me in utter disbelief and more than a fair share of disappointment.

"Johnny, if you stay here, you'll end up dead. You might not think it but those wings on your chest are incredibly valuable to this country."

"And the people buried under those buildings are

even more valuable to their families. I'm staying here, Mike. I won't hold it against you if you don't want to stay."

The latter part of what I had said had the desired effect. He knew that I would never hold it against him, but the insinuation that I would do if he was to leave me was far too great a risk for him to take.

"Very well," he said, unbuttoning his jacket, "but you're the one going to the CO about why we're late back."

"I think he'll understand, Mike."

He grunted as if to say that he wasn't quite so confident but was still more than happy to allow me to be the one to talk to him.

The low drone of engines, some more of a whine than a drone, slowly throbbed back overhead, as more and more ack-ack guns suddenly seemed to burst into life. The noise was fantastic and, had there not been so serious a threat, it all would have been quite enthralling.

"What can we do to help?!" I bellowed to the older man who had shared a cigarette with Mike.

He looked up at me, quite surprised that the two flyboys in front of him were so willing to help. He didn't seem to have all that much confidence in the RAF in the skies, but perhaps we would be able to restore some of his hope that we could still work hard on the ground.

"Davies Street has taken an absolute pounding. Hop on with those boys there from the AFS. They'll take you around. Be prepared to see some more bodies though boys."

Without another word, we scarpered over the rubble and debris that blocked our way, before climbing aboard what looked like an old single-decker bus, complete with hose reels to its rear and a water pump ready for action.

As we slid into the back of the cab, squashed to bursting with at least six other men, I heard a voice call out to us.

"Fank you, lads," the elderly warden called out, tipping the edge of his helmet towards us. As we trundled away from him, I was not quite sure if it was to the two flyboys who had just offered their assistance, or to the whole crew, who he might never see again.

As the bell began to sound, completely in vain against the plethora of other noises that were far stronger, I began to let my mind wander for the very first time that day.

I started to think about what I had just let myself in for, and what I had coerced Mike into doing. There was a chance that we could get killed here, and I had barely even allowed Mike the opportunity to get to a relative safety.

The young girl, who had held my hand so tightly that I thought I was her only lifeline, kept reappearing in my imagination, as I wondered whether or not anyone had had the courage to tell her that she would not see her brother in the morning. She would, in fact, never see him again.

As the thought came to my mind, there was a pang of guilt from deep within me, that maybe I should have been the one that had divulged the news to her. I had saved her life after all; we had some sort of a special connection.

But she was only a child, a young one. She wouldn't have understood if I was to simply tell her the news, especially when she was so excited to tell her brother all about her story. I might have felt a pull towards her, but there was no way that she would have appreciated the news coming from me as a result.

The journey to Davies Street could not have been more than a mile, but it took us almost twenty minutes to reach the site where it seemed a thousand bombs had fallen. There wasn't a single building in the entire street that resembled anything of a home.

"We start at this end and work our way down, alright? We don't move on until I say so, even when you start hearing them calling out. We have to be thorough here."

The officer in charge of us all was a stern-faced man, but one who quite clearly had the best of intentions at his core. It was a difficult job, but one that had to be done.

I hopped out of the cab, with an enthusiasm that was quickly quelled by the same thought that I had earlier on, but not had the confidence to voice.

"Mike," I said, gloomily. "My family, do you reckon they're alright?"

He sensed the panic in my voice and decided against a half-hearted response.

"Where did you say they were?"

"Richmond."

"I'm sure they'll be fine, old fruit. What is there that the Germans would even be that interested in, anyway?"

I wasn't sure. But I was scared for the life of my family all the same.

10

My body began to pulse with utter exhilaration as I tumbled from the aircraft. There was a strange feeling to it all. I was aware that I was falling towards the earth at an alarming rate, but at the same time, it did not feel quite like a fall.

It felt almost as if the wind was trying its hardest to hold me up, like I was in an open palm, being offered up to the gods as some sort of sacrifice. It was marvellous.

The wind rushed down the canals of my ears, twisting and winding their way down hallways and corridors as the air began to burrow into my brain. Had I not felt quite so weightless already, I would have been quite giddy and lightheaded.

I tried earnestly to move my head around, to rotate just a little, in order to see if I could make out the ground, or Mike. But there was no sign of either, although I knew of both presences.

Mike would be around me somewhere, completely terrified and yet wonderfully invigorated, as he made his way to earth.

I had relished in every second of freefall that we had been given, whereas Mike spent the whole time in a panic, a frantic worry that his chute would not open, only relinquished at the moment that the wind began to calm down tremendously.

He was always quite the worrier, was Mike, which gave him the awful tendency of opening his reserve parachute too early and putting himself in even more danger than he needed to. I, on the other hand, loved the feeling of rushing through the air, the overwhelming chill of the sky buffeting and bashing away at my eyeballs.

Frequently, I would leave myself far longer than I needed to reach for the toggle that would release my parachute. I liked it better that way. If I was to die with a failed chute, then at least it would all be over in an instant for me.

For a brief second, the tumbling figure, still dressed in the royal blue of the air force, his silk scarf flapping around in the wind fell just behind my eyes. For the first time since I had heard the news, I pictured Teddy Higgins' face as he rushed to the ground, the realisation that his life was to be over in the next few seconds.

It was a look of resignation, but also one of complete defeat. Shock. He knew what was coming, and he did not know what to say. Which, for Teddy, was an unusual phenomenon as he often spoke with such garrulity that it would frustrate the other chaps no end.

"Ah!" I screamed, at the top of my lungs, as I finally felt the piece of cord reach the end of the static line. One end, faithfully attached to the bomber from which we had fallen, had been yanked downwards, hard, which ripped the top of the bag that was strapped around my chest.

I had a brief moment of complete discomfort as I felt the bumbling mess above me begin to spread itself out, before a peaceful silence descended, with only the low drone of the Whitley engines moaning off into the distance.

There was nothing around me. There were no other sounds, there was no light from what I could see and for a fleeting moment, I was the only living creature on God's earth. Just me. What a thought.

I had often entertained the thought that I would very much appreciate being the last human to roam the earth. With nothing and no one able to distract me or make a noise that I did not want them to. I liked the idea of locking myself away in some ramshackle old shepherding hut in the Highlands, never having to see another person again if I did not want to.

I was aware that it made me something of an anomaly, as man has spent centuries trying to better connect himself with fellow man and here was I, desiring the opposite. It truly was a marvel that we could speak to another chap in America, thanks to the wonders of the telephone, but there was something innate in me that desired to be isolated, craved to be left alone.

For a moment, as I drifted through the inky black midnight sky, I dreamed of what it must be like on that evening, on the glowing sphere which was the moon. I wondered how peaceful it must have been up there, and whether he was taking pity on me, a lone man, drifting through the sky, who wanted nothing more than to be on top of the steely grey ball.

Maybe one day man might get up there, I thought. And maybe then I could have my peace and quiet.

Gazing from one glowing white mass to another, I searched above me to check that my chute was fully opened, as I didn't take much pleasure from the thought of ending up like poor old Teddy Higgins.

I was certain that the same sort of thoughts would be galloping their way through Mike's head, as we now gracefully fluttered to the ground.

It was this part of the descent, the slowest part, that always made me feel at my most vulnerable. We were dangling around in the sky, gradually making our way to the ground in the most conspicuous way possible.

All it would need would be for one lonely, desperate and slightly odd German to look up into the sky, towards the moon, and wish that he was there, for the whole game to suddenly be up.

As far as we knew, however, there ought not to have been too many enemy soldiers in this small region of France, particularly in the area that we were hoping to land in.

Restigné, the small village that we were slowly descending on, was a small, rural community in central France. There were few people there, which was both a blessing and a hindrance.

"The fewer people to spot us," Mike had chimed, when we had initially been briefed.

"But far easier to spot the outsiders, Mike."

"True, true," had been his melancholic reply. "How far from the *Loire* are we there?"

"About six or seven miles, I'd say."

Mike stared at me for a few seconds, waiting for me to spot the glaring error of my ways.

"Sorry Mike," I spluttered, my cheeks reddening the minute I began to correct myself. "Kilometres. About eleven or twelve kilometres. We'll be dropped just north of the river."

"Mistakes like that will get us killed, Johnny."

"I suppose it's best that I make them now, before it really matters."

"Don't make them at all, Johnny."

I had made them frequently, but fortunately only in private with Mike. It was as if he had some sort of nervy influence over me, like whatever I did mattered far more in his presence than with the officers who were in charge of our evaluation.

They could get me ejected from the course, and

back flying Hurries in no time at all. But Mike, it seemed, put a far greater pressure on my mental capability.

I watched with both astonishment and relief as the ground of *Restigné* came up suddenly to meet my feet. I pushed my knees together and squeezed, preparing myself to land and trying with earnest to remember everything that I had been taught.

"Slightly bend the knees. Then, when you feel the ground, tuck in, roll and flick the legs over to your right side. It distributes the impact far more effectively and will make your landing far more enjoyable and comfortable."

The look on the instructor's face told me everything that I needed to know. Even if I nailed every single one of his instructions, the chances of my landing being anywhere near comfortable were closer to zero than zero itself.

As for the enjoyable aspect, I found that, no matter how I ended up connecting with the ground, I found the whole experience utterly exhilarating. I was not so sure that it was the landing itself that had made each jump enjoyable, but the fact that I had made it, my skull and ankles completely intact, that I revelled in.

My last jump in, however, came to a swift and abrupt end.

Without much warning, my ankles gave way, rolling over in opposite directions, as I felt my knees buckle in a similar fashion. The crushing weight of my upper body collapsed in as much an undignified manner as my lower body and, before I knew it, my chin was slamming into the top of my left knee.

I let out a low growl as my teeth sank into my tongue, the odd twang of blood instantly rushing to my taste buds.

Instantly, my head felt like it was splitting in two, as a torrent of pain began to surge forward and engulf every inch of my brain.

Before I could feel sorry for myself, I had to sort out the chute. It was tugging away at my shoulders, the straps working their magic on the undersides of my arms and cutting them savagely. Slowly, like a rag doll tied to the back of a motorcycle, I bumped and smacked my way across the field, as the last few breaths of wind attempted to push the parachute as far as possible.

I tugged and pulled as much as I could, trying to dig my heels in like a stubborn child. Fumbling around as if I had forgotten everything that I had ever been taught, I finally remembered the small box that was strapped to the front of my chest. Hitting it as if swatting at a fly, I felt the harness fall away quickly and, as I wriggled free, I came to a halt, no longer at the mercy of the falling silk chute.

My ankles throbbed and I could already tell that they were turning a deep purple in colour. My tongue was dripping blood intermittently, forcing me to spit large mouthfuls of it away, while simultaneously wiping blood away from my nose, which had begun to bleed inexplicably. It was probably to do with the nerves.

There was no time to catch my breath or feel sorry for myself, so I quickly grappled with the parachute, bundling it back into my chest, until it was no larger than a two-year-old child.

It was only then, in the sickening silence that had enshrouded me, that I realised what an awful racket I had been making thus far. I had shown no real concern for the grunts and growls that had escaped my lips. Nor had I really attempted to quieten the chute as it had flapped in the wind.

I suddenly stood stock still, bolt upright, in the middle of the field, as I tried to listen out for anything that resembled something hostile.

There was nothing; no movement, no sounds, no features. It seemed as though this patch of land that I had bundled into was nothing more than a barren wasteland.

But then, as I strained, I could have sworn that I had seen movement. Straight ahead of me. There was no end to the field, no trees to mark the perimeter, not even a fence from what I could tell. I had no reference point for the movement, to the point where I was almost able to spin in a complete circle simply trying to find it again.

"You alright, *vieux fruit*?" He had been especially proud of himself for learning that phrase, having gone to our translator to determine whether it conveyed exactly the same meaning as 'Old Fruit' had done. "Blimey. Tough landing?"

I said nothing. I dared not even look at him. I simply stood there, parachute cradled in my arms, my nose and mouth staining small patches of it in scarlet.

There was nothing for a few more seconds. And then, I saw it. Definite movement.

I threw myself on the ground, the chute cushioning my fall wonderfully. I dragged Mike down with me. He knew to keep his mouth shut.

Not knowing if he could even see me, I stretched my arm out and pointed.

Then, there it was again. A lone figure, coming towards us. Armed.

11

As the shadow drew closer to us, I began to wonder whether it was a person at all, or if it could have been some sort of spectral apparition. But ghosts don't tend to laugh. Nor do they regularly acquire a *Karabiner 98 K* rifle.

I recognised the outline of the weapon, before I had even distinguished the features of the woman's face who was coming towards us. She was on our side at least, as I was still to hear of the Germans employing women in an anti-parachutist patrol capacity.

The rifle looked worn and well-used, presumably by whoever had used it prior to the woman who now stood in front of us, as I could hardly imagine that she had been engaged in as much fierce fighting as the rifle suggested.

The *Karabiner* was a sturdy, dependable weapon and had, in fact, been one of my personal favourites out of all the foreign weapons that we had tested in the North of England. It had a strange looking bolt attached to it, which seemed to droop downwards whenever it was pushed forwards. It was fiddly to reload, especially as it could only take five rounds at a time, and so you frequently spent your time pushing stripper clip after stripper clip into the internal magazine.

But it worked, and it worked well. Which is all that concerned me about the one that was slowly coming to greet us.

I flinched suddenly, as I watched it move quickly, as I pictured the irate farmer's wife, incensed that we would have the indecency to land in her field. But how would a farmer's wife have got her hands on a German rifle?

I opened my eyes, cautiously. The rifle was no longer in such a threatening position, as if it had been stripped of all its life-taking powers. The barrel was poking up from behind the small lady's head, like some sort of ant's antenna.

"You are my delivery?" She spoke in English, so perfect that for a moment I thought that the navigator had made a monumental error. Neither of us spoke, for fear that we had been set up in some way. It was always better, we had been taught, to say nothing, that way we were not able to incriminate ourselves.

But, on that night, there was no need. We were two men, both covered in bumps and scrapes, one of us still clutching to his parachute, like an overly-attached child. She had all the evidence that she needed.

"You are the men I was told to expect?" There was an agitation to her voice, as if we weren't quite what she had been hoping for.

"You'd better hope so, darling," Mike crackled, his throat as dry as mine from the jump. "Otherwise you're in for a very lengthy stay behind bars."

"*En français*," I urged, my blood boiling at the very fact that the two of them had even dared to use the English language. "Do you want us all to be killed?"

The woman chuckled, as she looked me up and down in contempt. "Relax, *plouc Anglais.* There is no one around here. We are quite safe."

"As safe as you can be in a country that is occupied by thousands of Germans?"

"Exactly," she smiled towards Mike, his sarcastic remark soaring over her head.

"So," I asked, "What now?"

She looked around her, as if expecting something to come creeping out of the darkness. But there was nothing but the silence and blackness of the fields around us.

"You must hide that thing, to start with, *lavette.*"

Mike chuckled at her second insult in as many minutes, "I don't think she's quite taken to you, old fruit."

"I do not take to anyone who thinks they are superior to me, just because I am a woman."

"I don't think—" I started, raising my voice

perhaps two or three decibels higher than strictly needed.

"Let's talk about this somewhere a little more… enclosed, shall we?" Mike suggested.

"Follow me, *crétins*."

"You hear that Mike? I don't think she's really taken to you either, has she?"

"Her loss," he mumbled, leaning into me so she could not hear. "I don't much fancy these French types anyway."

The woman sauntered with ease across the fields and the woods that she guided us through. Mike and I tripped and stumbled our way behind her, our heads up so that we could keep sight of her silhouette bobbing and ducking around branches.

My ankle rolled to one side and I ended up on my backside, a pile of dried leaves exploding around me as I did so. Mike helped me to my feet, as I heard the woman mutter under her breath.

"I*mbécile*."

Before too long, we found ourselves on a far sturdier track than we had done before, as the fields and forests began to thin out, as houses and shops began to appear.

"We are in *Restigné*?"

"No, idiot. This is Paris."

My palms grew moistened, and I rubbed my fingers into them to try and distribute some of the perspiration. I did not like it here, and not simply because it wasn't home. People were milling about, not many, but more than enough to notice that two new outsiders were making their way into the village. Their accomplice armed with a Jerry weapon.

"These people…Why are they not inside?"

"Most of them have jobs to go to. Others just do not sleep all that much."

I took a glance at my wristwatch, "It's four o'clock in the morning. Is there not a curfew?"

"There is. Of course, there is. But there aren't many Germans around these parts. There aren't quite enough of them, you see."

She spun round to face both of us, sensing the shock that was also etched across our faces.

"But, do not worry, *héros*. You will see plenty of them. Soon enough. Be patient."

The woman, who still remained nameless and aloof, had a spiteful streak to her, the kind that would pick on anyone, it seemed. I couldn't imagine her being one of the most popular figures in her local village, but that was probably what made her so good at her job. At least I hoped that it did.

She stopped abruptly at one door in particular and, without looking round to see if we were still with her, knocked with such a ferocity that I thought the door might cave in. I certainly saw it wince once or twice.

A middle-aged gentleman, dressed smartly for the time of day, peered back at us from the other side of the reeling door, before flinging it open, as if to greet his long-lost friends. He had a small, pencil-thin moustache, slightly skewed on one side as if he had in fact just scribbled it on in a hurry.

We filed in, as he shook and pulled us in to the warmness of his home.

"*Bonjour, bonjour, bonjour,*" he repeated, offering each one to the three individuals who were now stood in his living space.

Mike and I both replied, as politely as we could, before a moment of silence descended on us.

"Leave now, Alfred," the woman demanded, as she began to pull her shoes and socks off, perching on one of the rickety-looking chairs. "Sit," she insisted, without looking at us, proceeding to massage her feet.

"This is your home?" I asked, innocently, in an attempt to break the silence more than anything else.

"Of course not," she almost spat at me. "You really think I would live somewhere like this?"

I did not quite understand what she meant by 'somewhere like this,' but I took the chance to have a decent swivel around in my chair regardless.

The house was bare and rather non-descript, the walls a blank space, void of anything except a coldness to them that resembled our welcome. There was nothing really to it, nothing in the way of luxuries or comforts, and I wondered if she lived in somewhere far grander. But I gradually got the feeling she did not have a home of her own at all.

I noticed, perched on the mantelpiece above the fireplace, a small picture, in an unelaborate frame and yet, somehow, it caught my eye. It was unusual, I thought, to have a picture of such a young man and yet, not to have him proudly displaying his uniform. I rebuked myself suddenly as the thought crossed my mind that, Alfred's son, at least that was who I assumed it was, had maybe already perished before the war and as such, had not had a chance to do his duty.

But, as I looked away from the frame, there was something about that photograph, that made the face of the young boy seem even clearer than the black and white tones would allow. I could imagine everything about him; his skin tone, the way he spoke and the way he walked. There was something about him that would haunt me forever.

"So, are you going to tell us who you are?" Mike inquired, with a tone of accusation to his voice. It did not seem like he could trust her all that much. I was far more open-minded.

"You first," she stated. "After all, you are the foreigners here."

Mike went to argue with her, but I stepped in this time, trying to prevent an argument between the two of them.

"Jean. Jean Pelletier."

We both had new names now, new identities. We had lived with them for a good many months, in preparation for exactly this kind of scenario, and yet we had still found it exceptionally difficult to refer to each other by our new personas.

Jean Pelletier had been a soldier at one time, a

French one that had managed to make his way back to Britain via Dunkirk. He had died of his wounds shortly after, but his death meant that I had been given a new lease of life.

We had both retained our initials, and Jean Pelletier, in particular, was so close to my old name that it was hoped that if I signed something in my old one, my scrawling handwriting would be enough to confuse any inspecting police officer. The best way to avoid detection, however, was getting it right. Something that I was finding routinely difficult to do.

"And you?"

"Michel. Houdin."

Mike seemed in even less of a mood to play around and be polite than I was. The serious side of his face was quickly taking the rest of his emotions hostage. The tension in the room was more than palpable. Mike and I both despised the woman in front of us for her hostility, we were there to help her and her people after all. But she seemed to despise us because apparently, we had told her that we could do a better job than she could.

"And you? What is your name?"

"Suzanne Seguin," she muttered through gritted teeth, as she apparently discovered a knot in the arch of her foot. I wasn't sure if it was the pain that she had induced that made her speak in the way that she had done, or whether it was out of a genuine disappointment that she had had to give some information away.

The way she conducted herself was unattractive, ugly almost, but as I watched her, the creases and contortions of her face changing every so often, I came to the realisation that she could be quite attractive. She would need to iron out the ugly mannerisms and accusing glares, but her slightly freckled face was not all that unpleasant to look at.

She had long, flowing, blonde hair, that I was suddenly surprised hadn't lit our way while we were out in the fields. Her eyes, quite uninteresting and unremarkable, somehow demanded my wholehearted attention, to the detriment of everything else that was going on in the room.

Her voice, seemingly more pleasant now that I had noticed a softer side to her appearance, was sauntering around the room, like some sort of internal angel in my head.

"We will stay here a while. Then we will travel to another safehouse. Then you might get to see some Germans."

A door in the corner creaked open, causing me and Mike to spin suddenly in our chairs, reaching for our non-existent weapons.

"Alfred. If you are that inquisitive, why do you not come in?"

He hid behind the door once more, before he flung it open, clutching a bottle.

"It's a bit early for all that, don't you think?" I asked.

"We haven't been to bed yet, so I like to think of it as really late," Mike replied chipperly.

"Me too," replied Suzanne. It was the first thing that they had agreed on all evening. "Besides, we are occupied. All the rules are meant to be broken. You'll learn that soon enough."

12

"I hear that you are to be leaving us soon, my friends."

We both looked up, to stare at the old man that had been so hospitable to us in the last week or so. I stopped giving all my attention to the map that lay spread out before me, the unpredictable and intertwining lines making no sense to me whatsoever; without having been able to go out and pick out some of the local landmarks.

It had been a frustrating time, in *Restigné*, but one that I knew I should not take for granted. It was a small, farming community around there, where everyone knew everyone else's business, which was both a nice change to what I was used to, but also an indescribable annoyance.

The news of our presence had spread faster than cholera and, before we knew it, we were the recipients of every kind of gift, from bottles of brandy, to ancient-looking goats and sheep. The former was most welcome, but we knew that we had to be careful.

Drink too much, and in the wrong company, and there was a good chance that we would be arrested before we could even get to work. It was a very real eventuality, that had been drummed into us since our first day at the training school, and one that we both saw as less favourable than death itself.

We were here to do a job, and we intended to see it out as fully as we could.

"Where did you hear that, Alfred?" I asked, patiently, as he had been so with us. We had stayed in his house every night since we had arrived, escaping only for a few hours at a time to wander around the streets and begin to accustom ourselves with the French way of life.

"Suzanne told me. She has not told you?" he asked, quite innocently, but I caught his eyes defying him as they darted over towards the fireplace. I followed, my eyes instantly drawn towards the windows, as if I had the feeling that someone had been there recently, watching the three men sitting silently in the house.

But no sooner had I thought that the young, handsome man from the mantelpiece was calling me again, as if he had known my name. For a while, I thought I had seen something of Alfred in him and thought maybe that it had been a portrait of the man, in his younger days. But at the same time, there were remarkable features that set them apart, that convinced me enough to believe that this was Alfred's son.

"No, she hasn't told us," Mike said with a forceful aggression. "You just wait till I see her! Do we not deserve to be the first to know?!"

Mike flew from his chair, pacing the floor so much that I worried that the soles of his shoes would be worn thin.

I remained silent, opting instead to stare straight at the old man opposite me.

"I am sorry, my friend. I thought she would have told you by now."

I nodded in Alfred's direction, to acknowledge what he had said, but my mind was immediately anywhere but the room that I was in. I was concerned, so was Mike, but I was able to internalise my emotions and keep them to myself. It was a weakness of his.

The questions began to appear in my mind instantly, as my eyes fell on the window where I had been convinced there was someone watching. I could feel my thoughts becoming more irrational, as the paranoia grew, but I could see no other way of thinking.

Why had she not told us? There could have been a thousand reasons why, some more justified than others. Maybe things had not been finalised yet, in which case I could understand why we had been kept in the dark.

But why then had she told Albert, the middle-aged

man who, as far as I could tell, would have nothing to do with us the minute that we stepped out of his door for the last time? Why did he have a right to know something that we didn't?

Things began to add up to answers that weren't all in alignment.

I began to question Suzanne, and whether or not she was up to the job. She had been less than secure when coming out to meet us, nonchalantly wandering around the fields with a rifle cradled in her arms. Anyone could have seen that and tried to challenge us.

From what we could tell as well, she had not had anyone with her, it was just her alone that had come out to meet us. Which, in itself was a danger. But maybe it was because she did not like men telling her what to do that had made her opinion of security so lax.

The final question was that she had not bothered to check any of the codewords with us, the ones that we had been straining to remember for weeks beforehand. It was only at that moment that I realised that neither Mike nor myself had challenged her in her neglect, which made us just as culpable as her.

My mind began to play grand, elusive and elaborate tricks on myself, as I began to see steel helmets appearing at the bottom of the windowpane, as *Wehrmacht* soldiers crouched down to gain entry to the house.

The eyes of the young man on the mantelpiece

began to follow my movements and maintain his steely stare on me, as I imagined him in the crisp, black uniform of the *Schutzstaffel.*

We had been in *Restigné* for less than a week, but already I could feel each of my nerves being slowly shredded as if each one of them was slowly being frayed with every second that ticked by on the large clock behind Alfred's head.

"You are both okay, yes?"

"Of course, Alfred. Of course. There are just a few things about Suzanne that do not sit right with us. Do you know much about her?"

He shuffled uncomfortably in his seat for a second, before looking down at the ground. It was unusual, to see a man of his age and experience, being humbled in such a way by a woman not even present, who was young enough to be his daughter.

"She told me not to talk to you in this way. We could talk about anything apart from one another and our backgrounds."

"That's rather odd, wouldn't you say, old fruit?" He paced over to me, switching to a fast-paced English in an attempt to confuse our host. "She's quite happy to disregard blatant security measures when our lives are at risk. But the minute it comes back to her it's more secure than the Bank of England."

I looked across at Alfred, trying to read his face and work out if he had understood or not. His eyes, still staring down at the floorboards, gave me the impression that he knew he was not allowed to listen in.

"Alfred. Alfred, *regarde moi.* Look at me."

He did as he was told, his face completely forlorn. There was something in his eyes that told me that he was used to being ordered around, and would do anything that anyone told him, as long as it meant that he would have had an easier life. He would have made a first-rate footman.

"What do you know about her? Is she committed to her cause?"

"I have known her a good many years," he began muttering, ignoring the second, and more important question. He pulled out a handkerchief from his pocket and began rummaging away at his nose. It was an ornate article, with the letters 'A.S' stitched into it in a lavish red embroidery. It captured my attention, although for what reason I did not know. "I knew her parents very well. They lived here in *Restigné*. But then she moved away. To be married. That was a few years ago now."

"Why did she come back?"

"The same reason why everyone else began to move," he looked up, with a resigned shrug. "The war. She told me that she had been up on the coast somewhere and after the armistice, she came back. Wanted to be with her parents."

"Then why you? Why are we not with her parents?"

He sighed, "Hector and Esther Seguin died in the German bombing. Two days before the armistice."

"And she did not know?"

"Nobody thought that she would want to. She did not exactly get on very well with her parents."

"Why was that?"

"The same reason as I fell out with mine, my friend. We fell in love with the wrong people, or so our families thought. You see, both my family and the Seguin family were proud Frenchmen. They believed in marrying those of the same nationality."

Both Mike and I inadvertently shuffled to the ends of our seat, so that we did not miss another word that proceeded from Alfred's lips.

"I married an English girl," he said, looking up and into my eyes for the first time since he had started. "Her name was Helen. I always loved the way that you English people say it. The French way is so nonchalant, so…airy. The English way is far more pronounced. As if it means more to them. She meant a great deal to me."

His eyes were suddenly filled with tears and, although we were itching to know what it was he would say about Suzanne, now did not seem like the right time to press him for answers.

"Suzanne was young when she got married. Her family did not feel like she had thought it through entirely. I would suppose that they were right in one regard. He died in some fighting somewhere, I cannot remember where now. But, I suppose, if she had not married him, she could well have died in the same raid as her family. So, there is that blessing I suppose."

"Her husband, he was a soldier?"

"Of sorts, he was a—"

The lock on the door began to rattle viciously, as a key was thrust into the lock. As if he was petrified of what might lay in wait for him if he was caught, Alfred shot up from his chair, sending it scratching over the wooden floor, as he made a leap towards the sink. It seemed as if he was trying to distance himself as much as he could from us so that whoever it was coming through the door could do anything but accuse him of talking to Mike and me.

Sensing the fury that might suddenly erupt, I rededicated my attention on the map in front of me, as Mike opened his book up to re-read the same chapter that he already had done.

Suzanne stood in the doorway, her small frame somehow appearing far more threatening than when she had had the rifle in her grasp. There was something about her timing that panicked me, as if she had pressed her ear up to the keyhole to hear what Alfred had been saying about her, only to burst in at what could have been a vital moment.

The invisible eyes that I had been sure were observing us were beginning to form up in my mind. They were a steely grey, emotionless, and attached to the pretty face of Suzanne Seguin.

"We are leaving. One hour. Pack up everything

that you need. You will not be coming back here again."

I could tell that Mike was trying his hardest to act surprised, as if we didn't already know that we were soon to depart.

"That is a frightful shame," he began. "This is perhaps one of the most splendid hotels that I have ever had the pleasure to stay in."

He looked across at Alfred, who had turned away from the sink to face us, a big grin on his face.

"The pleasure has been all mine, gentlemen. I pray for your safe return. Maybe we will see one another again, someday?"

"Don't start all that Alfred. They will *not* be returning here."

I wondered how she could be so sure and questioned the meaning of her statement. Had she meant that we would not be coming here again, as we went about the pursuit of our duties? Or had she meant that we would not live long enough to be able to return?

Either way, there was only one thing that I was certain of. Suzanne Seguin was one that I could not trust.

13

Our journey to *Tours* was marked with a perfect silence, the likes of which I had never experienced in my life before. Not even Mike seemed capable of breaking it in order to confront Suzanne. She had an air about her that made it almost impossible to quiz her, to question why she had done what she did and her motivations behind it.

It was almost like we were both scared of her.

The silence in the car, a noisy but surprisingly comfortable Citroen, was broken only by a few coughs and splutters, mainly from its occupants, but worryingly from the engine also.

While we had stayed in *Restigné*, we had become accustomed to the French way of life, almost untouched by the occupation. However, the closer we got to our destination, *Tours*, the more we began to realise that our stay there was going to be one characterised by being in daily contact with our enemy. It was a fact that did not sit particularly comfortably with me.

We had been trained how to kill these men, whether it was with our bare hands or with a pistol or knife. We had undergone thorough training in how to communicate with them if we needed to, and how to identify various high-ranking officers and different regiments.

But each time we had been on an exercise, it finished, we were able to go home safe in the knowledge that we weren't about to be arrested or executed. But in *Tours*, there was no end to the game. We were, as the Major had put it, "actors in the largest play imaginable. A play in which the curtain will not be drawn for a good many months."

It seemed as though Suzanne had completely forgotten the fact that we were less than impressed with her performance so far. It was only because we had no other choice of what to do that we were even sitting in the car with her. If there was something else we could have done, we would have done it. But we needed her, and she knew that.

She smiled throughout the entire journey, occasionally waving to pedestrians and cyclists as we chugged our way down the main road into the city. It was like she considered herself royalty.

As we passed yet another Opel Blitz truck, mercifully empty of any troops, but still nonetheless occupied by a curious German passenger in the cab, Suzanne turned to face us.

"There are many like that. They will stare at you, try to break you silently. They can spot a spy from a kilometre away. They have orders to bring in at least one resistance worker a week."

"You can't possibly know that. How could you know that?"

"I have some very good friends, in some highly unusual places."

I suddenly felt the urge to ask about her husband, as I had the most peculiar feeling in the pit of my stomach, one that told me that she wasn't as pretty and clean as her appearance would have us believe. There was a dark side to her, an ugly side, one that had not truly reached the surface with us yet.

As I went to quiz her, she interrupted me.

"*Tours* is a dangerous place to be," she repeated. "One of your English agents was arrested only two days ago in *Orléans*. He made a very stupid mistake."

She spat her last few words, as if she was incensed that the English agent had been so foolish that it had amounted to a personal attack on her.

"What did he do?"

"He was crossing the road. He looked to his right before his left. There was a German watching his every move while he did it, apparently."

We thought for a moment, before Mike spoke, "Apparently? So, you didn't actually know this man or see it happen?"

"Well, no," she said, her body tensing up in

defence. "But I heard it from a friend in *Orléans*. So, you should be careful when you're here."

"Well, forgive me, but I'm not going to be taking too much notice about what your invisible friend says about our agents. Besides, we don't even know which sides your friends are on."

"What is that supposed to mean?"

"It doesn't matter," I butted in, trying to thaw out the frosty atmosphere that had developed inside the car. "The point still stands. We must be careful here if we do not want to be caught. How long until we arrive?"

"Ten minutes maybe. We will walk the last half a kilometre. Make sure you know where your papers are. If you fumble around for them, it will look like you are not used to producing them."

I pulled mine from the inside of my pocket and inspected them. A sharp, clear photograph of Jean Pelletier stared back at me. He looked tired, fed up and as if something was eating him up from the inside.

It wasn't far from the truth, and I could only hope that any inspecting German soldier would not be so analytical as I was. Jean Pelletier was a man that had made mistakes, and the brightness of his skin and eyes was due solely to the fact that he had been given a new lease of life, an opportunity to make amends for his past.

I forced myself to look away from the card and stuffed it quickly into my breast pocket. Instead, I began unbuckling the case that I had laid out on my lap. I began to run my fingers over all the different carpets that I had stored in there, as if trying to clean something from within its fibres.

The number of samples that I had in my case was overwhelming, to the point where I thought my arm would be wrenched from its socket the first time I picked it up. My cover, along with my sales partner Michel Houdin, was that we were travelling carpet and rugs salesmen, visiting various wealthy customers up and down France.

I had spent hours learning about carpets and rugs, from the cheapest varieties that I could get my hands on, to the rarest and most expensive Persian rugs known to man. If it came to it, I would try to talk my way out of an inspection with my overwhelming knowledge of the things. But I was hoping desperately that it would not come to that.

"Okay, we get out here. From here, we walk."

We stumbled from the car, my breath instantly eluding me as I heaved the case from the seat. I found it almost impossible to catch my breath again, as Suzanne was already striding out in front of us as if she was more than happy to leave us abandoned in the city.

As she continued to pace away, without looking back once, I began to think that, if I was unfortunately captured by the Germans anytime soon, I would be more than happy to give this woman's name up. But I had managed to convince myself that the

Germans already had her name and that she was some kind of *Sicherheitsdienst* agent, out to capture us in the most elaborate of plots.

I felt light-headed as I continued to struggle with my breathing. As I looked around at the city, with its marvellous cathedral dominating the skyline, I realised that this was it. This was the real thing.

There were Germans here, plenty of them, but there were also locals, locals that we would have to convince to be on our side. And I wasn't sure where many of their loyalties would lie.

Many, we had been told, had simply accepted the Germans being there, opting instead for a quiet life, rather than a free one and a large proportion were happy to keep it that way. If that meant turning over a couple of British agents, then I had been convinced that they would have no qualms in doing so.

As I managed to catch up with Suzanne, I caught the eye of a young German soldier across the road, his helmet attached to his webbing just clinking gently against the rest of his kit. I held his gaze for perhaps a second too long, in which time I managed to recall the way that Suzanne had suggested their tactic to stare an agent out was one regularly employed.

I felt like I had to look away, to break the deadlock and get on with my day. But I couldn't.

The German took a step forward, about to cross the road. He thought better of it as a truck, stuffed with troops, barrelled its way past him at a lightning speed.

Our eyes were still locked, even after the truck had passed.

Instead of crossing, to check my papers, the young soldier did something else. Something almost inconceivable. He nodded in my direction.

There was a brief moment where I connected with him, where I wanted to go over to him and talk to him. But the rational side of my mind prevented me from doing so.

What if he hadn't nodded at all? What if it was just my eyes playing tricks on me? There was a chance that he had mistaken me for someone else, one of his comrades maybe. He was not my friend, after all.

Nevertheless, I found myself bowing my head for half a second, as I nodded in return. Disengaging my eyes from the German immediately after, I rushed to catch up with Suzanne, who had ducked off the main road and into a side street.

I replayed the episode with the German over and over in my mind, even while we walked through the door of another middle-aged man, who bore a striking resemblance to Alfred.

"Ah, welcome, welcome. My friends," the man said, as he embraced us, kissing us on both cheeks. Mike reeled away from him, giving him both a quizzical and horrified look in equal measure.

"And you, my girl. How are you?"

"Very well, Monsieur Plantier. Very well."

I noticed that there was a frostiness in her emotions towards the man, which was not reciprocated by Monsieur Plantier. He seemed a welcoming and accommodating man, if not a little overbearing.

He showed us to our rooms and watched as we unpacked our few belongings, keeping certain things hidden from the man that we had only just met.

After a while though, he realised that we weren't about to build a bomb in his upstairs room, nor were we about to radio other agents to coordinate a large attack. Eventually, he became bored and left us to our own devices.

The pattern of being left alone continued for a week or so, as we spent our days milling around the streets, working out where local landmarks were and how to escape the city if we needed to.

As we took a right down *Rue Christophe Colomb*, Mike began to think of our latest escape route.

"Reckon you could swim across that, old fruit?"

I looked at the river ahead of me, not fast-flowing enough to drown someone, but quick enough to pull you a decent distance downstream.

"Not sure. Probably. Why?"

"On the other side is an island. Just trees and forest. If we're ever on a sticky wicket, I say we swim across there and lay low."

"Let's hope it doesn't come to that. It would take us ages to dry out."

"I think the possibility is far more likely than you think, Jean."

"What makes you say that?" I asked, turning to face him in the middle of the street.

"Our accomplice. The delightful *Mademoiselle* Seguin. I don't trust her."

"Me neither. I want to know what happened to her husband."

"I think I know," he muttered morosely. "I saw her being very chummy with a German officer yesterday. Particularly chummy."

"How do you mean?"

"Put it this way, I've been less friendly with some of my girlfriends."

"Why didn't you tell me sooner?"

"How could I? She's been in the house with us the whole time. Have you noticed how she never lets us out of her sight?"

"She's let us out now, hasn't she?" I asked, trying to convince myself just as much as Mike.

"That kind of woman doesn't have to be the one doing the looking to see things."

"You can't know that for sure," I mumbled, almost quivering.

"Look behind you, Johnny," he said, in unashamed English. "We've had the same young lad following us for the last three streets. He's either being paid by the Germans directly, or he's working for Suzanne Seguin."

14

The next few days were spent in almost total solitary confinement, as we silently pondered what we were to do about Suzanne. In our silence, we had convinced ourselves that she was not what she was making out to be, and her seeming unwavering patriotism was nothing more than a front, to make a profit out of both sides of the war.

"I reckon she killed her husband," Mike had suggested.

"That's if she ever had one in the first place. The woman seems like nothing more than a compulsive liar."

"I wish we could go and see Alfred again. I reason that he has all the answers we need right now."

We had considered bringing up the whole situation with Monsieur Plantier, the man who was accommodating us for the time being. He was a single man, with no wife or children to speak of and nothing to really show for his life except a pronounced limp from the last war.

But, on balance, it seemed like Monsieur Plantier, despite his best intentions, was not a man of great intelligence or awareness, and so reasoned that he would have had little understanding of our plight.

Suzanne came and went, informing us of the goings-on of her fellow fighters, as we counted down the days till we were due to contact London.

"Maybe she's not on the Germans' side after all," Mike managed to say through a cloud of smoke. "Maybe she's one of those communists. It would make sense."

"How so?"

"Well…they're not really on any side, are they? Except their own. It adds up with the fact that she's helping us to disrupt the Germans, but then making alliances with the Germans in order to further her own cause."

"I suppose that is a possibility."

"Besides, what other organisation would allow a woman to impose such fear and authority over others? Only the communists are like that. They even shake hands with one another."

"I don't think that is entirely a bad thing, Mike."

"Oh, come on Johnny. You don't buy into all that *'Bread, Peace, Land'* do you?"

"No, I don't, but sometimes treating everyone with the same level of respect isn't so bad. Just because she's a woman doesn't mean she's any less good at her job than us, Mike."

We had become used to switching between English and French while in Monsieur Plantier's house, as it meant that our conversations were more detailed and fruitful than if they had been in our second tongue.

But the boredom that had ensued, had meant that sometimes our conversations had moved away from what was strictly necessary and the close proximity to one another had led to some rather heated moments, surpassed only by the times that we continued to share with Suzanne.

"Michel, what will you do after the war?" Monsieur Plantier asked over a cup of coffee one morning.

"I will go home, Monsieur Plantier. I will pick up my life where I left it. This war is nothing but a minor interruption to me," he chuckled heartily, reciprocated by his host, before staring into the bottom of his mug, as if it was a window to what had once been.

"And you, Monsieur Pelletier, will you go home also?"

I stuttered for a moment, as my mind threatened to take me to a place that I would have rather not thought of. It was something that I had never considered, as I was not entirely persuaded that I would see it through the war. I thought talking of home would somehow curse my life and be sure to put me in the ground.

"I have no home to go to, Monsieur Plantier."

"No wife? No family?"

"No. None to speak of."

I sensed Mike bow his head in a moment of contemplation and embarrassment.

"I lost a lot of my own family in the last war," the kind-hearted Frenchman went on, clearly sensing my hesitancy to continue. "My father, two brothers, a cousin. All of them perished at different stages of the war. My mother too, a casualty of the war."

"She was a nurse?"

"Oh no. Nothing of the sort. She died of a broken heart. Mine too was broken, but I have been kept here on this earth for another purpose. I suppose you two are a part of it."

There was a soft squeal of brakes outside, as what I assumed was another German truck pulling up somewhere in the street, as they so often did. But there was something troubling Monsieur Plantier, his head cocked to one side, like a dog, noticing a difference to the normal pitch of the engine.

Without saying a word, his head still turned towards the front door, he stumbled his way to the front of the house, using the dinner table as a support for his stiffened leg.

I looked across to Mike. His face was not one of alarm or concern, but of dejection, as he continued to stare at the bottom of his cup.

"Oi," I rasped, kicking his leg under the table. He looked up, surprised. I nodded towards the door, where Monsieur Plantier was now peering through the small window at the top.

"Is everything alright, Monsieur?" I asked, with wavering tones.

"I am not sure. Wait a moment."

"What is it?"

"Germans, a lot of them. I think they are about to do a search."

"Do they do that a lot around here?"

"Not without reason. Even they don't bash doors down without a premise."

I looked back at Mike. His face was as ashen and scared as mine felt. We knew those soldiers were coming straight to Monsieur Plantier's door. And there was nothing that we could do to stop it.

"They are coming this way, my friends. Get your stuff and leave. Leave now!"

We shot from the table, sending the chairs in different directions, and the mugs crashing to the ground. We thundered up the stairs to gather our belongings, at which point we could already hear the fist thumping on the front door. Monsieur Plantier answered. There were voices. Muffled, but they were talking. Quite respectfully, for now.

I made sure that my suitcase was tightly secured, before checking the contents of Mike's for him.

"What are you doing?" Mike hissed.

"We have to make sure everything is there, otherwise our whole purpose here will be pointless."

"Let's get out first, then we can check it!"

"And find that half our kit is missing? Are you mad?"

I flicked the case open, to inspect the wireless set that it apparently tried to conceal. The suitcase itself was inconspicuous, but the sheer weight of the thing was more than enough to give you away if you appeared to look like you were struggling with it. It was why we took it in turns to carry the case, in the hope that a fresh arm would not appear so tired.

"The coils are missing!" I screeched, trying to convey the urgency while also hiding as much of my voice as I could.

"Forget it, Johnny. If we don't get out now, we'll be dead any second!"

"You go, Mike. I'll catch you up."

To my surprise, he turned towards the window, ready to throw himself out and escape in the agreed way. He flung the glass open, sending them smashing into the wall behind them, as I felt every pair of eyes downstairs suddenly look up.

I heard Monsieur Plantier say something, followed by a slight chuckle, as Mike prepared to leave me on my own.

Then, with a series of curses that would have made even the most seasoned of sailors embarrassed, he turned back towards me.

"If I get killed here, I'm blaming you."

Without another word, we began hurriedly searching the room for the missing coils, until they were found under Mike's bedframe.

"Come on, I'm not waiting for you now."

As the voices downstairs grew louder, Mike tossed himself from the open window, as I heard his body connect to the ground with a thump.

Acting as the only go sign that I needed, I heaved the more important suitcase up and onto the ledge, before dropping it down into Mike's arms. The case was far too heavy to catch properly, and I could see the rage and profanity in Mike's eyes as his arms were crushed beneath its weight.

After tossing out the other case, Mike moved away and into the alleyway that ran along the back of the houses in the street.

I pushed myself from the window, in much the same way that I had done from the Whitley bomber, landing far more gracefully than I had done the first time around.

We began running, just at the same time that we heard voices from the far end of the alleyway.

We daren't look over our shoulder to see who it was that was shouting, we already knew who it would be. Iron grey uniforms, with eyes as steely as the helmets on their heads, would be stood at the end of the alley, giving chase to the two men that were ahead of them.

"Halt! Halt! Oder wir schießen!"

It was too late for us. If we stopped now, they would shoot us regardless. At least if they shot us while we ran, there was a slight chance that we would be wounded, instead of killed.

Either way, there was something about the possibility of being struck in the back that I did not take to all that kindly. There was some sort of ironic cowardice in the act. We posed no threat to them whatsoever, and yet they would happily gun us down without even giving us a real chance to escape.

Most unsporting of them.

The brick around us began to crack and shatter into tiny little shards, as the soldiers behind tried their hardest to fire and move.

The alley was narrow and cramped but, as I played chase with Mike's back, I realised that, in a peculiar way, it played to our advantage. It meant that only one soldier could really fire at a time, unless he wanted to blast the head off the man who stood in front of him.

So, although the rounds were throwing mortar and red brick dust right into our paths, the volume with which that was threatening us was considerably less than it could have been.

We reached the end of the alleyway and, bursting out of the tight confines of the eight-foot walls, I drank in the comparative silence.

But, as I composed myself, I became aware that there were far more gunshots now that we were out of the alley, than there had been when we were in.

I chanced a look backwards. Just in time to see a lone figure, a man, dressed in black with a workman's cap on, peer out from one of the backyards. He had a rifle. The same rifle that Suzanne had had with her on the first night that we had met her.

He was taking pot-shots at the Germans, not really succeeding in hitting any of them, but doing a sterling job of keeping them off our toes.

I wondered for a second who had sent the man, or whether he had lived there by chance, but, as Mike tugged at my sleeve, I realised that it did not matter.

The fact was that he was there and, for now at least, we had been granted another opportunity to do what we had been sent for.

"That man!" I cried, "He needs our help!"

"What help can we give him, Jean?" Mike bellowed, already beginning to make his way to the river. "The best help we can give him is by staying alive!"

I went to argue with him but restrained myself. We would not be able to help the man, whether we stayed with him or left. But by keeping ourselves alive, there was at least a chance that we could help his fellow countrymen, his family possibly, to rid themselves of the Germans that were now descending on the poor man.

I turned, giving one final thought to our rescuer, just as I watched a round just clip him in his upper arm.

15

"I don't really fancy it all that much now, old fruit. How about you?"

"It's a lot further than I thought. Besides, how can we get this across without it being damaged?"

He thought for a moment, "I rather thought that we would have to escape without that thing, if truth be told."

We stood staring at the body of water, that seemed so flat that you could roll a marble over the top of it, wondering what we would do next.

The tranquillity of the water, the almost sedentary position that it adopted, was far from what was going on in my insides. My heart was still thumping out of my chest, my throat feeling as if it was trying to close up and starve my lungs of any oxygen. Sweat was rolling down my sides as it trickled from my underarms, and the perspiration on my forehead was enough to fill the river before us, several times over.

Our plan, to swim across the water, to the relative isolation of the island, was neither well thought out nor executed. Our failure to consider the one most important bit of equipment, other than ourselves, was enough to bring our egos crashing around our ankles.

"Now what?" I asked, as the sounds of rolling truck engines and general pandemonium continued to clamour around Monsieur Plantier's abode. "They'll be spreading their search soon enough. If they haven't done so already."

Mike looked around, erratically

"Come on, over here. I've got an idea."

Reluctantly, like a younger brother following his elder sibling, I trotted off behind him. Invariably, Mike's ideas ended with me either passing out blind drunk or standing in front of the CO's desk. On one occasion, I had found myself doing both. The CO was most unimpressed, it took him all of five minutes to reorganise his pen pot.

"Oh, and one other thing, Jean," he quipped, spinning around on his impossibly squeaky heel. "If we're ever in hot water like that again, we get out. No faffing around with that wireless set. We go. I don't know how many more of them I can take. Your problem is you're too straight. Always playing by the rules."

He muttered something else as he turned away from me, imaginably uncomplimentary, but at the same time filled with love and respect, as always.

He was right. I had nearly got the two of us killed.

The chances were, Monsieur Plantier would be killed anyway, regardless of if they had found a transmitter coil under the bed or not. He was replaceable. We were not.

But the wireless was a vital piece of equipment. If we had lost that, as well as our contacts, then we were less useful to the war effort than a wooden frying pan. In my mind at least, playing by the rules would pay off dividends further down the line. It was just such a shame that Mike's foresight went about as far as his charm did on the young woman tying up her boat.

"*S'il vous plait, Madame*," he begged, to the point where I thought he might cry. "My brother and I wish to scatter the ashes of our dear *mère.* She died in the most tragic of circumstances, she…"

I tried my utmost to maintain the smirk that was slowly threatening to give the game away. Mike went into such detail about how our beloved mother had passed away, that I thought even he had begun to believe it.

The girl, whose grand sum of worldly possessions lay in the boat, was stubborn, refusing to let Mike take control of the small vessel, even after he had fluttered a bunch of banknotes under her nose.

I couldn't help but let my mouth wriggle around for a second, as I tried desperately not to burst out into laughter. He had always fancied himself as a bit of a ladies' man but, here he was, failing miserably to even buy the young girl's affections.

Momentarily, the girl locked eyes with me, sending

a bolt of lightning straight through my chest. There was a second or two where I did not know how to react, the phenomena was one so strange to me that I had forgotten how one should behave around such girls.

She smiled at me mischievously, which settled my palpitations and perspiration no end. I was powerless to do anything except smirk back in her direction.

Without looking back at Mike, instead looking only to me, the girl snatched the wad of notes from his hand and tossed the rope in my direction.

"But…How? I mean, why? Why you?"

"It would appear, my friend, that sometimes a young lady appreciates a bit of honesty."

"But you didn't say anything."

"I didn't need to, Michel."

Mike spent the next ten minutes reeling from the fact that I had benefitted from a bond with the fairer sex that he simply found impossible to establish. I said nothing, apart from keeping the wry smile on my face, which seemed to infuriate him all the more.

It was a moment of contemplation for me, as we rowed ferociously towards the small island that inexplicably refused to move despite the metropolis around it. I hadn't experienced those kinds of emotions, the shockwave through the chest and the quivers of the heart for a very long time.

It was that calibre of reaction, the ones of the body, the ones that I could not control, that scared me the most. They were the ones that would give me away, but, more than that, they would be the ones that reminded me.

"Hey," Mike's voice suddenly resonated, as he slapped me on the leg. "Don't dwell on it. Not now."

I didn't even need to ask him.

"Your face. It goes grey. It gives you away. It scares me."

"Sorry, Mike."

"Don't be. It wasn't your fault. But don't let it distract you. Alright, old fruit?"

I nodded, as the bottom of the boat began to scrape and slide over the shingle that told my tired arms it was time to stop.

In silence, we began to heave the boat further onto the island, so that we could be safe in the knowledge that the boat wouldn't suddenly begin to float off on its own accord.

We had barely said a word about what had just happened, instead opting to ensure that we were as far away from the chaos as was possible. In the event, it wasn't necessarily the distance that made us feel safe, but the opportunity of concealment.

It would take a German with a good pair of binoculars and an unusual hunch to take a look over at the island and, with any luck, he wouldn't be able to see the two of us hunched behind the undergrowth.

The commotion had died down slightly, but it was more down to the fact that we were a decent distance away from the epicentre that we had the luxury of peace.

As the wind continued to breathe around us, letting up for nobody, I could have sworn that I caught the occasional German word, the odd command, as rooms and houses were upended, in search of the two men.

"What do you think we should do now?" I asked, hoping that Mike's own thoughts had been more fruitful than my own.

"Not really sure, to be truthful. We could radio London. They might have an idea."

"I reckon they'd have several. None of them any use to us right now, I'd say."

He hung his head as if he was in complete shame.

"Oh, come on, old chum," I said, trying to feign optimism and hopefulness. "It's not all bad."

"How so?"

"At least we don't have to stomach any more of Monsieur Plantier's coffee."

He chuckled gently, plonking his backside down on a tuft of grass.

"That's true," he said, finding the energy to look up at me. "It really was awful stuff, wasn't it? Reminded me of the stuff that Teddy Higgins used to drink."

His head bowed again, as he inevitably recalled the fateful day where Higgins had baled out of his Hurricane, his parachute failing to open. I couldn't imagine what Mike had seen on that day, no matter how many times I dreamt about it.

The more I looked at him, the more I realised that we were both damaged. We had been damaged by different things, but the same awful war.

"Come on, old fruit," I said, putting my frankly terribly impersonation of him on. "It wasn't your fault," I mumbled, returning to my own tones at the sound of myself.

"I'll tell you one thing about all this," he said, dusting off his clothes but still keeping himself firmly planted on the floor.

"What's that?" I breathed as I squatted down to join him.

"I will never trust that blasted woman ever again. I knew there was something about her. But I didn't think she'd try and hand us over that quickly."

"We don't know that it *was* her," I jumped in, defensively. "It could have been a random search."

Mike scoffed, "I know that I can be an unlucky so-and-so, Johnny. But that simply takes the biscuit. How many houses are there in *Tours*? You are trying to tell me that out of all of them, the Germans pick the one house that happened to have two British agents in?"

Instinctively, I looked around me, seeing nothing but undergrowth and insects to hear Mike's revelation. I just had to hope that they weren't German insects.

I let his blood cool for a few seconds before I

joined in the debate, trying to add a rationality to our thinking that even I was struggling to comprehend.

"Mike, there could have been a hundred other reasons why they chose Monsieur Plantier's house."

"Pray tell, Johnny," he said sarcastically, an arm waving out in front of him in submission.

"Monsieur Plantier for example. How do we know what he's been up to? He could have been out every night the last few months, laying mines and blowing things up. He could have been on the Germans' watchlist for months.

"It could have been something as trivial as not adhering to the blackout. Or refusing to give up his seat on the bus for a German.

"They might not have been looking for us at all."

He perused my weak and ill-thought-out suggestions which, surprisingly, he seemed to take more seriously than I had done.

"I suppose that you could be right, old fruit. I am rather glad I'm here with you, you know. You always were the cool one. If I was here on my own I rather suspect that I'd be dead already."

"Don't be stupid, Mike."

"No, really. I mean it."

I felt like blushing, but all I could really bring myself to do was to close my eyes, just for a brief moment. For a fleeting second, I was back in Cornwall, at Telwyn Farm, lying in the stream appreciating every bird and creature that sung above my head.

It felt like a lifetime ago, one where the memories had already begun to soften at the edges and recollections had faded. But just as easily as some memories had paled, others had sharpened, developed over time.

Just as Mike was fighting off the demons that beckoned him, complete with nightmares of a tumbling Teddy Higgins, so too were mine coming to fruition.

"It is strange though," he started again, hours after we had finished our initial discussions.

"What is?"

"The whole thing. Suzanne met us on her own. Why didn't she have anyone else with her?"

"Maybe she wanted to go on her own?"

"Or maybe she didn't particularly want anyone knowing we were coming? That way she could shop us to the Germans that little bit easier."

"But people do know that we're here. Alfred and Plantier know."

"Convenient for her though. Choosing the two men that seem utterly petrified of the woman."

I mulled the idea over some more. He was right. There were things that did not quite add up.

The way that she had left us for such long periods, the not informing us that we were due to move, the way in which that no one seemed to know all that much about her and were reluctant to tell us if they did. And, perhaps most curiously of all; she had been seen fraternising with the Germans.

"You're not going to try and convince me that all is well again, are you, old fruit?"

"No, you're right. There is something worryingly irregular with Suzanne Seguin. But I do have one thing that you're not going to want to hear."

"Oh?"

"We need her now. More than before."

16

"How are we going to find her?" Mike asked tentatively, as he strained under the effort he was exerting.

"I don't know yet. I'm sure she'll find her way back to us, one way or another. She seems like that sort."

He thought for a moment, as he carried on working away like a persistent rodent, trying to make his way into the pantry for a midnight feast.

"I'm not quite as certain as you on that front, old fruit."

"Why not?"

"She seemed pretty aloof to me. Secretive. And now that she tried to get rid of us, I'm convinced that she'll be lying low somewhere. Out of our way. She'll know that we want to have a stern word with her."

"We still don't know that it was her who told the Germans."

Frequently, I found myself getting defensive of

Suzanne, despite the fact that I did not trust her in the slightest. In fact, I would have wagered that I trusted her less than Mike did. But there was something about the whole situation, and Mike's frame of mind, that convinced me that I would have to persuade the both of us that she wasn't as bad as we had been making out.

"And you have no evidence to prove otherwise."

I looked at him triumphantly, as if I had backed the prosecution barrister into a corner that no one could escape from.

"But you, similarly, have no evidence to redeem her."

The prosecution counsel was back on top.

I rubbed away at my forearm, the itching that I had experienced before reaching a crescendo in the last few days, as I inevitably ran out of the ointment that I required to soothe it.

"It's bad?" Mike asked, nodding at my scratching. "I've noticed you doing it a lot more recently."

"Yeah," I replied. "It's getting worse. I need to find some sort of ointment that will help sort it out soon. Otherwise I'm scared I'll wake all the Germans in France up with my scratching."

He chuckled, softly.

"Want to talk about it all yet?"

"I can take a turn carrying that, if you want."

He stayed silent, frustrated at my lack of a real acknowledgement of his question. But through my own refusal to answer, he had received the most complete answer that he could have expected from me.

As we continued to walk through the wooded area, I knew that he was thinking of exactly the same thing. He had been with me the entire time that the event had unfolded.

I pondered how he had seen things, if he had different memories of that night compared to me, as it had not affected him in the same way that it had done in my life.

He must have been saddened by what he had seen, I don't think anyone could have been hardened to the goings-on back then, but he had somehow managed to carry on.

Just days after it had all happened, he was back with 249 Squadron, flying sorties over the skies of Kent, as the Germans refused to back down on their plan to eradicate us all.

Meanwhile, I had run away. I had run away from everything that I could have taken comfort in, run away from all my responsibilities, but perhaps most importantly, I had run away from the war.

I had wanted the end of it all. I did not want to see another rifle or bomb blast ever again in my life. I craved the silence that only a peaceful nation could offer, the solace of the birds flying through the trees and insects going about their days uninterrupted.

You never seemed to get any of that in a war-torn city.

I knew, of course, that you did, but it was never the same, it never had the purity of true peacefulness.

Everyone knew that I had gone AWOL. Everyone on the Squadron knew that I had left them, without so much as a farewell or an explanation. But, for some reason, they had all understood. Even the CO, which was unusual for a man like him, so often a stickler for all the rules.

It was why I had been allowed to stay at Telwyn Farm, almost completely uninfringed, as I began to become accustomed to the way of life down there; one where there was no war on.

I was ashamed that I was there, more because of who I subsequently became associated with than anything else. There were men there, men of fighting age, who too had run away from their responsibilities. Their responsibilities to join up and fight.

It frustrated me, to hold the knowledge of what other brave men were doing, while there were some who buried their heads in the sand and lived a life of luxury out in the country. It angered me all the more to know that it was only the wealthy, only the ones who had a full pocket of notes, that could afford to do so.

But still, even while I was there with these detestable rats of society, I did not think of myself as one of them. None of them could even imagine what I had been through, mainly because I refused to tell any of them.

I was petrified of them going to the police and

revealing who I really was, forcing me back into the life that I had run so far to avoid.

In reality, I was just as bad as them, abandoning the chaps who were fighting the hardest battles and burying my own head in the sand. In many ways, I was even worse than them. I had made some terrible mistakes that had led me to Telwyn Farm.

I thought about how long I would have continued there, if the police officer had not turned up requesting my presence. I liked to think of myself as a better man than the others at the funk hole, that I would have eventually returned to 249 Squadron and resumed my duties there.

But, deep down, I knew that that wouldn't have been the case. I would have carried on there until the day that I died, if I had been able.

In many ways, the phone call that Detective Sergeant Calhoun had received had saved my life.

I had never been inside a police station before in my life, and there I found myself, for many hours, sitting at the desk of the local inspector, as he frantically began trying to get through to the man who had summoned me.

"Flying Officer Parker?"

I confirmed my name, with the most crackled voice that I had ever heard, as if it was being played out through a wireless set that had not been tuned correctly.

"My name is Captain Langham. I need you on the very next train to London. Do you understand?"

"Yes, Captain. I understand."

I waited and waited for the inevitable revelation that I would hereby be placed under arrest and escorted back to London by some of Cornwall's finest officers. But no such revelation came.

Only an address. And a time. And Flying Officer Michael Hope's name.

The phone line went dead. I was then handed a train ticket for an hour's time, alongside a small card, which repeated the address and time.

"I reckon here is as good a place as any," Mike's voice spoke, as he interrupted my meanderings. "Johnny?"

My body shuddered as I tried to bring my thoughts out of the past and into the present.

Michel was stood before me, the old royal blue uniform that he had once proudly worn, now replaced by the underwhelming clothes of a French labourer.

His face was darkened further than usual, on account of the lack of moonlight that was able to make its way through the treetop canopy above us. It was what had made it perfect for what we were about to use it for.

Mike ran his hand through his floppy mop, trying to replace a wayward streak of hair that was defying the order to stay flat to his scalp. His hair was always inch-perfect, but not tonight.

It seemed a little more ruffled, rushed even, which was reflected in the slight stubble that had begun to sprout over his chin. But even so, despite his dishevelled appearance, looking more like a vagabond than a soldier, his eyes continued to glisten, alert as ever, and his warm smile was still enough to light the way of my feet.

"Yeah. I should say so."

"Good. Then let's get cracking."

He wasted no time at all in flicking open the catches on the large suitcase, before fumbling around with a key to open the lock. Looking up at me with a mischievous grin, he flicked the case open.

"Here we go then. This is when the real work starts."

"So up until now has all been a test run?" I scoffed.

"We've passed so far. Wouldn't you say?"

He chuckled away to himself as he observed the equipment that lay before him. Without hesitation, he began pulling and tugging at rolled up pieces of wire, expanding them out full length before even starting to put the stuff together.

I watched him as he plugged in the coil that we had so nearly left behind, as well as the batteries and headset. Finally, he plugged in the Morse key and the antenna, which was wound tightly on a thin piece of card, which he passed to me.

"Here you go. Make yourself useful. Nice and high."

I took it from him, and began unwinding it, looking for a branch that seemed suitable.

"Oh, but not too high," he muttered, "Remember that we need to get it down again."

"Yes, I know," I said with agitation.

"Good. It's just I know how terribly awful your arm was back when we played cricket. Don't want a repeat of any of those misfields now, do we?"

I tried to take some comfort from the fact that he was enjoying himself, but I simply couldn't. We were about to transmit a radio message back to London, which was, as I reminded Mike, deemed an enemy country. An act which could get us shot if we were to be caught.

"Lighten up, would you?"

I couldn't help but be as serious as I was, as I was truly petrified of what might happen to us, as I began to see figures moving in the midnight trees. There was no explanation at all as to why we were out here this late at night, apart from the fact that we were enemy agents preparing to contact our headquarters for orders.

Mike, on the other hand, seemed freed by the fact that we were finally getting to put into practice exactly what we had spent months training to do. It just worried me, however, that his joviality could quite easily lead to a slip up in procedure, missing something perhaps that was standard protocol, all because he was too busy having a good time.

As a result, I watched his every move; from moving the tuning dials around to the desired frequency, right up until the point that he was ready to transmit. Fortunately, I could not spot any errors.

His lack of mistakes, however, was not enough to quell the paranoia that was burning within.

"Relax, will you?" he said, as he watched my head spinning on its axis like an owl's. The more that I looked, the more I managed to convince myself that there was someone out there, watching us, waiting for us to simply switch the set on.

I recalled the night that we had landed, when Suzanne Seguin had approached us out of the darkness and how, by the time that we had spotted her, it was already too late to run and hide.

That was exactly how I was feeling as I watched Mike sitting by the set, finger poised over the Morse key.

"Thirty seconds," I said, looking down at my wristwatch.

"Alright," he replied, as he fumbled around searching for the piece of paper that he had prepared his transmission with.

"Right then, Mike. That's one-thirty exactly."

"Okay, old fruit. Let's hope they jolly well answer, eh?"

17

The 'dits' and 'dahs' of Morse code was something that managed to confuse me no end. I had mastered it eventually, but that was in a training environment, where lives did not necessarily hang in the balance.

But, out there, in a dingy forest in central France, lives most definitely were at stake. Namely, Michael Hope's and John Parker.

It was why, after a little negotiation, that Mike had taken the reins on the wireless transmitter, as it meant that we had a reasonable chance of deciphering the message and staying alive for as long as possible.

I quickly glanced over Mike's shoulder as he prepared to send his message. It was a complicated code, worked out using two numbers that we had been given before we had departed. If we had forgotten those, then we wouldn't have been able to contact London at all. Not without breaking so much cover that even they would have to run for their lives.

Mike started tapping out the first few letters to London. Circuit Fortunae was in full flow.

The wireless operators back in London would then take our coded message, use the same two numbers, only working backwards, to reveal the message that we had sent them.

"That's the security check done," Mike said, peeling his headset away from his ear for a moment. "Now for the main show."

Despite his earlier enthusiasm and ease, it appeared that the situation was getting to Mike, a thin bead of sweating just dribbling over the precipice of his nose. His hands too were clammy, as I watched them briefly working their way over the surface of his trousers, trying to rid himself of even the slightest reminder of his nerves.

We had decided on our message earlier on in the day, in a graveyard of all places, as it gave us the best excuse of being somewhere, but also afforded us a little privacy to talk freely.

Due to the urgency with which we would need to send and the length of time that it took to decipher a coded message, we could only really afford to send and receive one message per night. If there was a requirement to talk more at length, we would simply have to do it over several transmissions, which could quite easily take days.

We simply did not want to be stuck in one location, with the set switched on, while the Germans were around. They apparently were in possession of highly-sophisticated range-finding equipment, that meant that they could listen to and locate a sending transmitter within twenty minutes.

Looking at my wristwatch, I could see that we had already spent ten minutes, and we had only just completed the security checks.

"I'm going to go further down the track," I mumbled into his ear. "Keep a watch."

"Don't go too far."

"Why, will you miss me?"

He chuckled softly, before flapping me away with his hand. Forcing the paranoia and apprehension down to the pit of my stomach seemed like the best way to go; Mike's perspiration had already seemed to slow.

Crouching low, making sure that my footsteps did not make too much noise or disruption, I made my way down the path that ran about twenty yards or so from our sending location.

There was a slight bank, which I hoisted myself over, which would allow me to look further down the track and spot any unwanted visitors sooner rather than later.

I lay flat on my stomach, allowing the midnight chill to really pierce through into the centre of my bones. Propping myself up on my hands, I felt quite comfortable, not in the conventional sense, but comfortable with how I was.

I was in pain, the cold chill merging well with the scratching arm and attacking thorns, but that suited me just fine. It seemed almost like a punishment to me, one that I deserved and gladly took upon myself.

I had made mistakes in my life, and now I felt like I was repaying that debt.

The paranoia was slowly subsiding, as I stared straight down the track for what felt like hours, not seeing a single living thing, not even some kind of woodland creature, scurrying around, foraging for food.

There was no one coming.

I closed my eyes momentarily, the lover's embrace of my eyelids returning for a meagre moment.

I thought of my childhood, my home, my family. There they all stood, shoulder to shoulder, staring back at me with the cheesiest grins stretched out across their faces. My father, a Major in the Last War, was a proud man, standing taller than all the rest while somehow being a good six inches shorter than my younger brother.

I looked at each one of them in turn, taking in the features of their faces like I had never actually forgotten them. It was difficult to see them, because of the haze, which had descended around them like a curtain of mystery.

But, at the end of the row, there was one, unmistakable figure. I could not make out the face, nor the features, but I could tell, by the way that she stood, the way that she held herself, that it was my wife.

She stepped forward from the cloud, as a

rumbling thunder suddenly began to bellow behind her.

Reaching out to me, I could hear her speaking, but the words were muffled under the sound of the thunder, which sounded more like a motorbike roaring in earnest than a furious Mother Nature.

Then her voice, more decipherable, yet still obscured by the belch of thunder.

"John. Look up, Johnny. Look up!"

Her voice turned into a shriek, as I shocked myself awake, my head bolting upright, just as the motorbike flew past me, a passenger in the sidecar.

The lights blinded me for a moment, as if I was watching some sort of heavenly apparition, my eyes taking a few seconds to adjust before they were assaulted again, but this time by a larger, more formidable light. The lights of a truck.

The squeal of the truck's brakes told me everything that I needed to know. We were in trouble. Serious trouble.

Every instinct in my body told me to leap up and run, run as far away from these soldiers as I possibly could. But, as I saw more and more of them pour out of the back of the truck, equipped with torches, I knew that my best friend right now was the darkness.

A light beam was flicked on, testing the strength of the torch. I buried my face in a pile of leaves. The light glanced across the ground directly in front of me.

You fool. You fool.

I berated myself over and over again in my head,

as I realised that I had allowed my mind to wander off, so far away from this land that I had forgotten the true perils that I was vulnerable to.

You fool.

More than that though, I had allowed myself to let my guard down. I had fallen asleep. I had let Mike down. We were going to be killed.

I looked across at the soldiers, all young men who took their task with little sincerity, which infuriated their commanding officer.

One young boy, holding the torch under his chin, lit up his face in a ghostly way, his face becoming more akin to a gothic statue than a human. A volley of laughter petered out and, as one slapped the torch from the young boy, the light momentarily bounced off the face of another.

A face that I recognised. It was the face of the German soldier that I had made eye contact with when we first arrived in *Tours*.

My heart was uplifted for a moment, as if there was a vague possibility that, if I was to be caught by that man, then maybe there was a chance that he would let me off. But I knew how futile a thought that was. I was being wishful, childlike.

I needed to change the way I was thinking. I needed to act in the way that I had been taught.

The men milled around for a moment, as the commanding officer stood with the man in the motorcycle sidecar. There was a problem, as the man gesticulated as if something was not working.

Hoping that it was the equipment that they were using to locate Mike and his set, I took my chance. All the lights were off. The men were smoking and chatting. I needed to move now. Fast.

Slowly standing up, I crouched, as if I was simply relieving myself in the undergrowth. But, as soon as I was able to turn, without too much noise, I did, half-sprinting, half-tiptoeing my way back to Mike. It caused an excruciating agony, but I had done the easy bit.

I kept my eyes strained for Mike, as my feet began to bellow in pain to stop. But I kept going. There was a more urgent need right now.

I ran around for what felt like forever, encircling the place that I had been convinced I had left Mike. But he was nowhere to be seen. Mike was gone.

My breathing began to falter, as the mucus at the back of my throat suddenly threatened to turn to bile. I was all alone. I was weapon-less. And there were twenty German soldiers no more than two hundred yards from where I stood.

Still, with no real direction or conviction, I ran around, my senses heightened as I hoped to see the back of Mike's head as he made his getaway.

Suddenly, I felt my head bash against a tree, a hole immediately opening up allowing blood to gush forth from it. A great weight landed on me, in a perfect rugby tackle that sent me straight to the ground, with my assailant on top of me.

I crashed into the ground with an almighty

impact, as I felt the wind knocked out of my lungs and the leaves blown from the trees.

"You shouldn't have done that, Johnny. I panicked. I'm sorry."

The weight on my back was instantly lifted and, as I fought with earnest to retrieve the air lost from my lungs, I found myself staring at the darkened, moody features of Mike's face.

"What's all that about then? Running around like a cow at the slaughterhouse."

"The…track," I gasped, each syllable a frightful agony to my chest. I struggled to get anything else out, but I only needed one more word to pass over my lips, for him to spring into action. "Germans."

He stared at me for a few seconds, as if he didn't quite believe me, which I did not blame him for. I was uncertain that I would even trust myself after what I had just done.

But, soon after, he was bundling the kit up, hauling things around to get them all back in the case. Finally, he unhooked the aerial from the branch that I had strung it up over and, without rolling it back up neatly, bundled it back into the case with the rest of the kit.

By the time that he had finished packing up, I was able to breathe again, albeit with considerable difficulty and pain.

"The message. What did it say?"

"Priorities, Johnny. Come on, we need to get out of here, now."

"Where are we going to go?"

"I don't know. And I don't much care. But come on!"

There were voices now, behind us and, as I looked behind, I could just about make out the first few beams of light just dancing off the trees some way behind us.

Picking up the case, I checked to make sure that we had left nothing incriminating behind us in the leaves.

"Come on then," I said puffing as I heaved the case over my shoulder. "I'll carry it first, then it's your turn. Lead the way."

Like a pair of naughty schoolboys, we began running away from the scene of the crime, hoping that the bruised lungs would be the only injury that we sustained that night.

18

"Johnny! Let me take over!"

I could not find the energy within myself to argue with him any longer, as my arms burned with such a fierceness that I thought they would give way at any moment. I had carried the case for what felt like days, but had, in fact, been merely an hour.

I dropped the case where I stood, from such a height that Mike thought it pertinent to open the case and double-check that nothing had been smashed.

"Are you okay to carry on, old fruit?"

"Yes, I'm fine," I replied, shortly, annoyed that he had assumed that I was anything but prepared to carry on.

"That's alright then. We've got a long night ahead of us after all."

Without any other options for us, apart from wandering around *Tours* until we found Suzanne again, we had decided between the two of us that we would head back to the only other place in the whole of France that we had any friends at all; *Restigné*.

There, we would see a few friendly faces, faces that we recognised at least, despite the fact that we were still outsiders to them. At least there, there were considerably fewer German soldiers, which meant that we would be able to recuperate there for a while, reorganise our thoughts even.

We had another time for a radio communication the night after, at two in the morning, which with any luck, would be considerably easier to carry out than it had been in *Tours*.

All we had to do now was make it through this night and get to our destination.

I felt happy that we were going back to *Restigné*, as it had become a sort of safe haven in my mind, one where I could not imagine any danger or threats, and where I could see myself staying for quite some time.

Locating the river *Loire*, we stopped for a moment, behind a series of hedgerows that seemed to grow all around this part of France.

"Have you got a light, old fruit?"

"Do we really have time for you to take a smoke?"

"Not for that, Johnny. For the compass. I can't see a damned thing."

We fumbled about together for a moment as I searched for a light, and he for his compass.

"Right then," he said as the small flame lit his way. "We need to head in this direction. South-West, along the river. Hopefully we begin to recognise some things along the way. When we get to that old barn, we'll know we're in *Restigné*. Looking forward to going back?"

"I didn't think we would be back so soon."

"Neither did Suzanne. It seems like everything she says we will do ends up going the opposite way, doesn't it, old fruit?"

"Yes, I suppose it does. Every time I think of her, it reminds me of you."

"What? Why?"

"Not sure. I suppose it just about sums up your luck with women, I suppose."

"Here, you're not far wrong with that one!"

It was the last conversation that we would have for quite some time, as we trudged our way through the fields, making sure that the river was always on our left somewhere. We desperately needed to know where we were, and that we weren't simply going around in circles. At least this way we would know if we were going in a complete circle because our feet would end up being wet.

We stopped for a moment, a welcome one. My feet were burning with exertion and my chest was not faring much better either. The dampness of the night was seemingly getting to my lungs, making it near on impossible to breathe.

I looked across at Mike, who had just finished relieving himself at the bank of the river. I could tell that the walking was taking the same toll on him.

He plonked himself down next to me, flopping himself out onto his back. He sighed.

Even in the darkness, I could tell that something was bothering him, his eyes already filling up with unexplained tears.

His voice, normally loud and gravelly, perfect for Shakespearean theatre, took on a different tone, one that seemed to inflect downwards in line with his disappointment.

"When you were a flight leader, Johnny."

The question seemed more like a statement, and I wasn't entirely sure if he was requiring an answer or not. Instead, I responded only by flooding my mind with the memories that I had.

Trundling down the runway together, with five other glorious Hurricanes, then lifting from the grass one by one and just clipping the treetops at the end of the airfield. It gave such a rush, such an exhilaration. So much so that one could almost be forgiven for feeling utterly invincible.

The power in the Hurries was like nothing that I had ever experienced before, each time my head smashing into the padded cushion behind my head, as my entire body was taken by surprise yet again.

There was nothing more overwhelming than the feeling of flying together, in formation, banking and climbing in perfect sync with one another, before landing in unison back at base.

But that was before the war started. That was before I started to return with only five kites in my formation. Sometimes four, sometimes three. On a rare occasion it was just me and one other.

"Did you ever lose someone that you felt awfully responsible for?"

"Of course I did," I said without any kind of hesitation.

"No…What I mean is, did you ever feel like you could have saved them?"

Many times. The name Rawlinson came into my mind. He was young. Perhaps only twenty-two or twenty-three when I met him. He was an eager Pilot Officer, ready to take on the Luftwaffe and shoot every last one of them down.

It was on his first patrol that I watched him go down. A ball of flames and smoke. He hadn't had the chance to bale out. He was most likely dead a few seconds after his aircraft had first been hit.

He had dived on a Heinkel 111, on my orders, but he went at an odd angle. I watched as instead of approaching directly from the rear, he approached slightly off to the port side, allowing the rear-facing turret gunner a clear field of fire.

I noticed his mistake almost immediately, but instead of issuing another command to dive or disengage, I instead decided to open up on the 111 that was by that time directly in front of me.

A few short bursts later, and I had scored another aerial victory. But Rawlinson had lost his.

His engine was ablaze, and I could hear his screams as he went down in a blazing fury. I had whipped my flying helmet from my head. I did not want his howls in my ears for any longer than they had needed to be.

"Yes. Many times. Why are you saying this now?"

He waited a few moments, before propping himself up on his elbows.

"I think maybe, Johnny, that I am cursed."

"You? Why, of course, you are. Look where you are!"

"No…I mean it, Johnny. I think I am a curse on our time here."

"Don't be such a fool, Mike. It's not your fault that things have gone belly up."

"I fear they are. As a punishment, you see. Teddy Higgins…"

"There was nothing you could have done about that, Mike. It was just the luck of the draw. We lose men all the time like that. It is a sad reality."

"Johnny…You don't understand. I *could* have saved him. When we scrambled that day, to fly over Maidstone…I took his parachute. It was on the wing of his plane and I took it."

"Why?"

"He already had one on. My one. He went and took it earlier in the day. He was joking that it would give him good luck, wearing my things. So, he sat in the thing all morning. That parachute, that failed to open, it was mine. I should have been wearing it. He should have been wearing his own one. He could have still been alive."

I did not know what to say. It was a natural risk that came with being a flight leader that you would feel responsible for the men that you lost, but for Mike, it went deeper than that. Teddy Higgins had died as a result of a failed parachute. The very parachute that Mike should have been wearing.

There was no way that Mike could have known it would fail to open. But that did not mean that he could have no feelings of guilt. There would now be a family without a son, all because he was joking around with another man's parachute.

He carried on, "I just don't know how—"

"Shh. Be quiet."

He looked at me with a shocked expression on his face at first, but slowly, as I raised a finger to my ear, he began to tune his ears to the noise that I could also hear.

There was a motorcycle. And there was a truck coming up close behind it.

"How on earth—"

"It doesn't matter," I screamed. "We need to find some better cover!"

Hauling the suitcase up onto my shoulder, we began to run, for the second time that night.

For a moment, I found myself wondering if it was the same group of soldiers that had located us in the forest as before, or if this was a different group of men. If it was the same, then I hoped that they were as tired as we were, and that their eyes were not up to standard for spotting two shadowy figures in the darkness.

But the darkness was not preserved for long, as the motorcycle suddenly angled itself in such a way that Mike ran straight into its beam.

He was seen instantly.

His initial reaction was to duck down, as if it would somehow keep himself hidden for a little longer. But it was far too late.

Men began calling out from behind us, as Mike picked up his pace and began to run for his life.

"Take the case!" he cried, "I'll draw them the other way!"

He ran away from me, and out onto the road, carrying on in the opposite direction to the now screaming soldiers behind.

"I'm coming with you!" I hollered back, not really knowing what else he was expecting me to do. There was nowhere else left for us to run.

The first gunshot sailed high over our heads, which I could only presume was a warning shot. It was that or the soldiers had been out of bed for far longer than I previously assumed.

I prayed that all the others followed in a similar pattern. I was not so lucky.

The second and third ripped just over the top of my left shoulder and I felt the fourth thud into the ground just ahead of my feet.

The next few were directed straight at Mike.

As I ran, I forced my head up, to see what it was

we were running towards, and if there was anywhere about that we could hide. I could see nothing.

But then, as I was beginning to feel myself slowing down, a pair of headlights suddenly flooded the road from ahead of us, the occupant clearly waiting for his moment to flick the switch.

Both Mike and I slowed, accepting our fate and awaiting our arrest. The motorcycle behind us began to roar once again, as it had done earlier on, as it closed in on us. So did the vehicle dead ahead of us.

As it came closer, I stopped, refusing to let go of the suitcase that I was prepared to guard with my life. I could make out the shape of a car, just over the top of the headlights, which were aimed lower than the truck's, so that it did not light so much of the way.

Suddenly, the brakes were slammed, and the vehicle stopped just short of Mike and me. We waited, to see the officer step out from behind its doors, pistol drawn, ready to take us into custody. But no officer came. Instead, just a simple command.

"Entrer!"

Get in.

No sooner had the man spoken, then there were bullets once again flying around our heads, as the men behind suddenly realised that the vehicle ahead was not one of their friends, it was one of ours.

With renewed vigour and optimism, we launched ourselves into the back of the car, landing on top of one another and cracking our heads together. The door hung open as the car began to manoeuvre around, and rounds began thudding into the bodywork, making the most spectacular of noises.

Within seconds, the car was screaming at the top of its lungs, hitting a phenomenal speed. The driver flicked the lights off, before yanking the wheel over to the right and into a field. Still, the man kept his foot depressed on the accelerator, with such stamina that I wondered if he had feet at all, and instead simply had slabs of meat.

We were thrown about the car wonderfully, as we barrelled our way over the field, and I could only imagine the horror that this farmer would be faced with, come sunrise.

Eventually, it seemed that the man could no longer keep his foot pressed on the pedal, as he began to ease off and, for the first time, he spoke.

"Are you two alright?"

"Have the Germans gone?"

"Yes, my friend. It would appear so, for now at least."

"Then, yes. We are alright," I said, finally answering his question.

"Who are you?"

"Don't you recognise me, my friends? It's me!"

He leant around from the steering wheel, to reveal his face, his old, stretched face.

"Alfred?"

"Yes! My friends! It is Alfred!"

"Thank you, Alfred."

"It is quite alright, my friend. Although, I am not

so sure how I am going to explain the bullet holes to Monsieur Genet."

"Who?"

"The owner of this car."

I felt like throwing up but with a smile on my face. My feet no longer burned, and my head no longer pounded with the force with which I had connected with Mike's own.

"We're alright, Johnny! We're alive!"

"Yes…"

My voice trailed off, as the feeling of vomiting suddenly reached my head. How had he known to come and get us? And how had he known where we were? I felt uneasy, and not for the first time that we had arrived in France.

"Alfred, what were you doing there? At this time of the night too."

"I was told to. I was on my way to *Tours* to find you. Apparently, you were in trouble."

"You could say that," Mike interrupted.

I ignored him, "Who? Who told you?"

"Who do you think, my friends? Suzanne. Suzanne Seguin told me to."

I looked across at Mike. His face was as puzzled as mine.

19

The forest that surrounded us gave off the impression that everything that happened within it was a total secret, shut off and hidden from the outside world. I felt as if I was in some sort of secluded retreat, where mythical creatures arose from its depths in the dead of night.

They didn't, of course, and I should know, as we had spent the night lying in the same patch of foliage that we now occupied.

It wasn't comfortable, which was probably just as well, as if it had been, there was more than a slight chance of either of us dozing off. We had tried our best to clear our patch of ground of dried twigs and leaves, but there always seemed to be one defiant weed that was intent on cutting our stomachs open to investigate our insides.

The discarded leaves and branches were piled up in front of us, to the point where we could no longer see over the small bank of rotting woodland that we had built up. That was fine, as we could still see through it at various points, which allowed us to keep a watchful eye over our target area.

The hope was, at a glance anyway, that we were nothing more than an unthreatening bush at the side of the wood, no cause of concern or need for investigation.

The deadwood around Mike began to rustle slightly, as he wiggled himself closer to me, leaning into my ear without taking his eyes off whatever it was he was focusing on.

"So, what do you reckon?"

I knew what he was referring to, it was all he had spoken about for the last couple of days. But still, I did not feel like giving him the immediate satisfaction.

"I reckon that I am going to be asleep within the next hour if something doesn't happen soon."

"No, I mean—"

"I know what you mean," I interrupted, not wanting him to repeat what he had repeated a hundred times already.

The truth of the matter was that I was as in the dark as he was. There was no way of really knowing what was going on in Suzanne's head. It seemed that even Alfred, who had claimed to have known her for some time, was none the wiser over what it was that she wanted in her life.

There was a large proportion of my mind that warned me that she was evil, not in the conventional sense of the word, but she was someone who for some reason enjoyed being on no side in particular, causing havoc for as many people as she could.

She had certainly done that already. We had been in France for less than three weeks and already she had been responsible for us being chased from a safe-house, having informed the Germans of our whereabouts.

There was also an element of suspicion about how the German radio finders had found us so efficiently. I had managed to convince myself that she had disclosed a time and date to her German counterparts to assist in our capture. It was a notion that I had not yet shared with Mike.

On the other hand, she had displayed some signs of loyalty, which dispelled my fears and attributed the misfortunes that we had to bad luck. Without her, Alfred would not have come looking for us, and instead of carrying out our order from London, we would be in some damp, stone-walled castle somewhere, which now belonged to the local Gestapo.

No matter how hard I tried to convince myself that she was in fact on the same side as us, she was our London-given contact after all, I could still not bring myself to tell her what it was we had been ordered to do. This had many of its upsides, one of which being that I felt secure in what we were doing. No one else knew where we were or what we were planning to do.

But there were far more pitfalls. It meant that we

were on our own. We could ask for help from nobody. It meant that our cache of weapons extended only so far as a sharpened branch, that Mike had fashioned out of boredom through the night.

And I didn't much fancy charging at an MG34 with a three-foot-long sharpened twig.

"So then," Mike repeated. "What do you think we're going to have to do?"

I ignored him again, which did not seem to ruffle him as much as it did other people. I supposed, being an only child as he was, he had grown used to it, with nobody else to talk to as he grew up apart from his own reflection and imaginary friends. It was more than likely the reason why he had made up for it in his adult life so far.

Instead of answering him, I pondered the events of the last few days, trying to conjure up some sort of context to the answer that we were both still searching for.

Alfred had taken us back into his fold and had spent the following days tending to our every need and request. We had asked for everything, from food and water, to a host of names where we could go if we needed a friendly face. A friendly face that was not his.

I had spent many more hours poring over maps of the local area, as well as *Tours* itself, in case we were ever required to go back there again. I hoped not, as I was convinced that the German soldier who had seen me when we had first arrived there, would have recognised me as the same man that he had chased through the woods that night. But I had no way of truly being certain.

The picture of the non-uniformed young man that sat atop Alfred's fireplace, had stared at me for so long that I felt as though I had got to know him in those lonely few hours, as if he had been sat in the room with me the whole time. There was something about that boy, that face that was still bewildering me, that drew me to him every morning that I entered the room, and every evening when I retired for the night.

I stared down at the road, just poking a finger through the bundle of twigs that lay in front of me to get a clearer view.

The forest in which we lay, just inside its perimeter, slowly sloped downwards, towards the road, which had been carved straight through the middle of the forest. The road, which bent and weaved through the forest, had been constructed deliberately for one man. According to Alfred, it had been built when he was a boy, by an eccentric businessman from *Lyon* who wished to escape the hustle and bustle of city life.

He must have been an eccentric, as he had only built his reclusive getaway about ten miles from another city; *Tours*.

Even still, had it not been for him, then the Germans would not have had a grand house in which to house some of their staff officers. But there was one officer in particular that we were interested in, the very same one that had been communicated to us from London a few days before.

There had been no time to engage in a coherent conversation with London, but a couple of messages on either side had been received and decoded in the short window that we had. During our next transmission, if we lived long enough, would be the time that we could reply to London's messages, and they to ours.

We had informed them that we had landed safely and had been to *Tours*, only to have been compromised soon after. We were now back in *Restigné*.

In return, we had received news of the grand house that we now sat near, as well as the name of a German officer. *Generalfeldmarschall* Hugo Sperrle, *Luftwaffe*.

He was due to visit the area in the next couple of days, London did not know when, only that he was arriving. It was our task to find and eliminate him.

Subsequent enquiries had found that he was in command of *Luftflotte* 3, the fleet of aircraft that had swept from Germany and into mainland Europe during the *Blitzkrieg* back in the previous year. He was an influential man, one who would have met with Hitler on numerous occasions it seemed, and one whose head would become a trophy if we managed to take him down.

We had had no opportunity to turn the operation down, or suggest any kind of amendments, and so we subsequently got to work, armed only with a sharpened stick, to take down one of the most heavily guarded men in the whole of the *Luftwaffe*.

I took a deep breath in, the warm air clinging to the inside of my mouth like some sort of glue, as I prepared to finally acknowledge Mike's question with some sort of an answer.

But, as I went to speak, I was interrupted this time. Not by Mike's voice, but by the growl of an approaching vehicle. As the noise matured, into a throbbing rumble, I realised that the motorcycle was not approaching alone. There were at least four other vehicles behind it from what I could make out.

Then, as we both peered through the cracks in our hide, the first tyre of the motorcycle came into view down on the road. There were two occupants, one on the bike itself, the other manning the obligatory machine gun in the sidecar. Neither seemed all that interested in what might be going on in the forest that towered either side of them, complacent enough to assume that no one would dare to strike in this part of France.

As the bike drew level with us, the open-topped Mercedes suddenly chugged into view, with another following close behind. Each vehicle had another three uniformed men inside, each one with more golden embroidery on his shoulder than the last, we could see it even from the distance at which we sat.

"That has to be him," Mike muttered his voice crackled and parched. We had run out of water at some time around five o'clock in the morning, and its effects were beginning to make themselves aware by now.

"Got to be," I replied, surprising him with the sound of my voice.

We watched as the other vehicles passed by, each one chugging along louder than those that went before, with every occupant completely disinterested in the trees that surrounded them, high on every side. Within seconds, they had reached the bend in the road at the northernmost point of our vision and had turned it without much drama.

"Well, that's that then, old fruit."

"One thirty-three. Now we wait to see what time he leaves again."

"Hopefully he leaves with less of an escort than that. Otherwise, there's no way that we will be able to get close at all."

"True."

As I finished my uttering, I looked across at Mike. His wide-eyed glare that seemed to want to swallow me down told me everything that I needed to know. He had heard something.

For whatever reason, I had not heard it the first time, but the second time there was no mistaking it. Someone was approaching us from the rear.

We lay there for what felt like hours, not daring to move for fear of making far more noise in the process.

My eyes were locked onto Mike's, which stayed as wide as they could go. There was so much eyeball showing that I marvelled how they were even staying inside his skull.

As I risked my first breath in what felt like an eternity, another noise began to waft to my ears. An even worse one.

Whoever it was that was approaching us, was doing so with a heavily-panting dog. Either that or the person was incredibly ill.

20

Mike's eyes widened to the point where I thought that they might just roll out onto the ground in front of him at any second.

We were going to need to move at some point, the footsteps and panting were getting closer to us. Soon they would be tripping over the legs that stretched out behind us.

The small gaps that were still present behind Mike's bulging eyes, suddenly filled with water as he began to panic. I did too but could only feel my heart intensifying as an indicator of my fear.

Thoughts began to flood my mind of what would happen if we were caught, from being interrogated about what I knew, to facing down a firing squad in a dingy courtyard somewhere.

Neither prospect really appealed to me, and so I found myself slowly rotating, to lie on my side and look back at what was approaching us.

It was just after one o'clock in the afternoon, and the sun was just over halfway through its day. It was good news for us, as it meant that the approaching figure would have to battle with the falling sunlight before he could make out what was in front of him. That too and the fact that the thick canopy of trees above us was enough to give off the impression that we were sitting in the middle of a solar eclipse.

My stomach gave off a dull ache, as the numbness that had accrued over the last few hours, slowly gave way to the rush of blood that I had allowed into the front of my body. It felt warm, to finally have some of the scarlet liquid rushing through me once more, but I became acutely aware that it felt like I had relieved myself into my own trousers. I did not have time to check whether the sensation was real or not.

We were covered by a series of trees to our rear, but even through them I could see the occasional flash, as a uniformed body made its way over to greet us. I cursed the dog that was at the end of its leash, as I was certain that without it, the handler would never have wandered this far towards the perimeter of the wood.

It was too late to try and make a run for it now. The figure was close, close enough to make out the rifle that he had slung over his left shoulder. If we were to up and run, with numb limbs and panicked hearts, there was no way that we would get much further than thirty yards or so.

I strained my eyes for a moment, trying to see past

the figure and his hound, in the hope that I could push them from my consciousness, just for half a second.

I desperately wanted to see if anyone else was with the man, maybe staying back on the track so that the dog could relieve himself with a relative peace and quiet, but I could not see anyone. It struck me as odd that a dog and his handler would be out here alone. There must have been a second figure out there, somewhere.

The figure began to whistle, just as the crunch of his boots began to be heard without the trees to soak up the noise. He was now practically on top of us. The dog's saliva would dribble onto my head any moment.

Then, I caught sight of the man, his nostrils flared, cheeks puffed out as he breathed out his tune. He was ugly, not the kind of man that I figured would be pictured on any of *Herr* Hitler's posters anytime soon.

He was tall, but from where I was laying, I figured that even a mouse would seem tall at this point. He continued to stare straight ahead, ignoring almost everything that his dog was doing, even oblivious to the fact that it had just been rugby tackled by St John's college's finest scrum-half.

I leapt up, coming almost face to face with the man straight away. The horror in his eyes was a little delayed in appearing, as I imagined the questioning thoughts that barrelled through his head.

How had he missed us? How had he allowed himself to be so stupid?

I slammed my forearm into the bridge of his nose, as I felt it crumple under the force, the blood taking a little longer to rush to it than I had anticipated. His head lolled backwards for a second, before shooting forward again, as my knee connected with the inside of his groin.

The head was the subject of my attention again as my knee connected with his face somewhere, which returned him, for a second, back to his normal, upright position.

He staggered backwards, pulling me with him and, as he fell, he managed to move himself out of the way of my falling body. My face connected with the ground first, landing on a dried log that disintegrated as I fell on it. A splinter must have embedded itself just above my eye, as a warm liquid began trickling into my eyebrow over the next few minutes.

I rolled over to one side, coming face to face with the barrel of a German *Karabiner* 98 rifle. I stared down it, marvelling at the preciseness and flatness of the barleycorn sight at the front of the rifle. I knew that these rifles were impressive, I had fired some captured ones back in training, but I had never truly been this close to the end of one.

It was only from this point of view that one could truly marvel at the ingenuity behind one of the most spectacular killing utensils that man had ever created. I could only hope and pray that this one had somehow developed a fault, that would prevent around becoming lodged in my brain. I was hoping for some kind of human error. The man behind the rifle looked too scared to pull the trigger.

I gripped the barrel of the rifle with such force that I surprised even myself. I was suddenly filled with such strength that I believed for a second that I would be able to bend the barrel upwards, if that was what I had wanted to do. But I couldn't.

Instead, I began heaving at the rifle, pulling it into me and trying to wrench it from the German's grip. He began to grunt as he fought back. I too let unnatural noises pass over my lips.

I roared as I pulled the rifle into me, rotating my body around as much as I could in the process. But still, the German clung on.

My hands suddenly lurched upwards for a moment. The gunshot felt as though it had ruptured my eardrums. I felt the round just whisper past my cheek as I lay there, boring itself into the nearest tree trunk that it could find.

It was the best thing that could have happened to me. I knew that, as long as I kept a firm enough grip on the rifle, jostling it around as much as I could, the German would not be able to slide the bolt back and home again to make the rifle ready. It was one of the major downsides to a single-shot, bolt-action rifle.

With as much force as I could muster, I pushed the rifle back towards him, the butt connecting with his lower jaw with a sickening crack. I repeated the procedure two or three times before I was satisfied that he was dazed enough.

I sprung to my feet, my legs burning under the duress that I had put them under. Still, the young German tried to pull the bolt backwards, but my influence continued to make him incapable of doing so.

The gunshot may have alerted everyone else to a situation going on in the woodland, but it had almost certainly saved my life.

I continued to jostle for the rifle for a few moments longer, pondering what my next move would be. I could not stay like this forever. One of us would have to give up eventually. One of us would have to die.

It was a strange feeling, to be fighting for one's life. It has an urgency to it that you do not get in any other situation in life. An almost super-human strength suddenly comes to the fore, taking even you by surprise as you fight off the threat.

But it also stops you from thinking too much. You do not think about dying, you do not think about what happens next. But you also do not think about how you will end it.

Thankfully, Mike was doing that bit for me.

As if from nowhere, he lunged at the German, bundling on top of his head like an overexcited child. He lay on the man for a few seconds, as I felt the resistance at the other end of the rifle slowly growing weaker, until there was nothing left. The rifle was mine.

Mike lay atop of him for a few moments more, panting harder than the dog had done, and far harder than I was. I was still in fight mode; my body was not yet crying out for the nutrients that it so needed to recover.

Finally, Mike slid himself off the German, leaving his body crumpled in a heap next to the unfortunate man who had stumbled upon us.

I felt sorry for him, as I stared at his lifeless corpse. It was just bad luck that he had ended up dead. It was just good fortune that had dictated that there would be two of us against one of him. If it hadn't been for his dog, then I did not suppose that he would have found us at all.

At the thought, I looked at Mike, whose eyes were now so full of tears that they had begun drowning, returning to their normal size once again. His pupils, however, were wide, as if they had been painted on by an over-exuberant artist.

"The dog?" I panted, my body finally catching up to the exertion that I had just been through.

He stared at me, as if I had lost my mind, and that the hound that had come panting through the trees was merely a figment of my imagination.

"Down there," he said, pointing back towards the road below. Sure enough, the dog was there, charging his way back up the hill towards us, never faltering in his impressive display of power and stamina.

"He's coming back. We need to get going."

"Of course, he's coming back."

"What do you mean?"

"I threw him a stick. He's bringing it back again."

"You're pulling my leg?"

"Straight up…old fruit."

Sure enough, as the dog got closer to us, a stick was duly hanging out of his mouth, ready to be thrown again. It was having the time of his life.

"We better clear up. Someone somewhere would have heard the gunshot. And we can't guarantee that the person will be friendly to us."

"Are there any of those around here?" Mike questioned, with a smirk on his face.

I ignored him, as I slung my rifle proudly over my shoulder, and got to work.

It was the first time that I had really taken note of the fate that had befallen the German soldier. Until that point, I did not know what it was that I thought had killed the man. But now, I could see it, as clear as day, and as proud as a mother of her new-born baby.

The sharpened twig, the one that Mike had spent hour upon hour sharpening with a stone throughout the night, was firmly placed into the neck of the German. The dried, brown leaves that became his falling place were quickly soaking up the scarlet liquid that leaked from the single wound in his neck. It was a deep red, a mesmerising pigment that would have been quite beautiful had it not been for the tragic circumstances that it denoted.

"I told you it would come in useful," Mike announced, as he tried to wrench it from the German's fleshy grasp, to no avail.

We began to strip the body of anything that might be useful to us; a small hunting knife, a pistol and a single hand grenade that had been hastily tucked into his leather belt.

Hurriedly, as we heard the screams of engines beginning to fire up from the mansion, we decided it was our time to leave. We were going to have to abandon the rest of our reconnoitre and try and take out the *Generalfeldmarschall* with a handicap.

It was what we had become good at, after all.

21

The atmosphere was frosty, to say the least. It was the first time that we had seen Suzanne since we had been forced to run from the safehouse in *Tours*, and she had not even expressed any regret over how it hindered us so far.

She seemed far more concerned with the fact that we could have led the Germans straight back to her.

There were a thousand and one questions swimming about somewhere in the silence, but it seemed like each one of us was as stubborn as the other, as nobody even uttered a syllable for what felt like hours.

Only Alfred, the elderly gentleman, in whose house we resided, had any kind of confidence to talk, offering cups of substandard coffee, or a biscuit that seemed to have been buried in his cupboards for generations.

The picture of the young man refused to take his glare off me, and I wondered if I would ever find out who he was, and why he had decided to latch onto my memory as he had done. It was one of the questions that burned within me, more than the ones that I had prepared for Suzanne, but there was something holding me back, as if I already knew the answer, but was not quite prepared for it.

"So," Suzanne began, making me jump in my seat. It had been so long since someone had spoken that I had begun to forget what a human voice even sounded like. She stopped for a moment, as a truck passed by the windows of the house, her eyes tracing its movements, even when it was obscured from view.

The paranoia in me told me that it was another German truck, searching the houses in *Restigné* after another tip-off. The water-filled eyes of Mike told me that he was thinking the same.

But the truck rumbled down the road somewhere, and the recognisable squeal of brakes, followed by shouted orders, did not come. Not near Alfred's house anyway.

"What is your plan?"

I looked across at Mike, whose moody face seemed moodier than ever. It was as if someone was shining a light behind his head, casting long and drawn out shadows around his eyes, which were filled with a sadness that had taken on a renewed purpose in the last few days. He had lost something while we had been out in the field, something that had silenced him considerably.

There was no mistaking what it was, I could practically see the tumbling body of Teddy Higgins at fifteen thousand feet, as Mike pushed the control column down to see if he could somehow catch him. I winced as I thought of his body connecting with the ground, at such a speed that I was sure he would have punched a mighty hole into the earth.

Mike had lost his cover, the façade that he had been building up over the last few months. It was gone now. He had revealed his secret to me, and I could tell that he was concerned about what I now thought of him, as the man responsible for Teddy's death.

But that was the last thing that had been occupying my mind. Each and every time I thought about it, my mind quickly diverted to *that* night, the one where my eyes had seen things far worse than Mike's ever had.

He had been with me, of course, but it's odd how what one man sees can affect another so drastically differently.

I looked back towards Suzanne. She needed her question answered, otherwise she would know that we were hiding something, and that could lead to further trouble down the line. Besides, there was no refuting the fact that we would be in desperate need of help, from her and her friends.

"The chateau, about fifteen kilometres from here." It had taken me a while to get used to it, but I was finally using the correct unit of measuring the length of things. Although he was dead against what I was saying, I knew secretly that Mike was impressed that I had remembered.

"*Château de Serrane*?"

"That's the one."

"What is your concern there? It is only a resting place for *Luftwaffe* junior officers who are recuperating, is it not?"

"Yes, it is. But they have a special visitor. The commander of the air fleet. *Generalfeldmarschall* Sperrle. London want him dead."

She gave it some thought.

"Why?"

Mike, renewed of confidence and sarcasm chimed in. "It probably has something to do with the fact that he is a high-ranking Nazi official. That would be my best guess anyway."

She decided to ignore his outright impertinence, as she so often did. It was probably why she had managed to make her way to become London's contact, as it seemed like nothing anyone said could deter her from what she wanted to do.

"So, what is your plan? How do you actually propose to take this man out?"

Mike suddenly exploded, unable to keep his emotions in check any longer. It was a trait that was a dangerous one, but for now, inside the relative safety of Alfred's home, it was one that could be expressed.

"Are we all just going to waltz straight past the elephant in the museum?!" I turned to look at him. As well as being into the historic literature of our home nation, he had too tried his hand at that of the Russian variety, where he had discovered the works of Ivan Krylov, a fabulist from some one hundred years before.

He had tried to entice me into his works, unsuccessfully, but not before I had read *The Inquisitive Man*, in which the protagonist wanders around a museum, taking note of all the tiny, minute animals, but missing the large white elephant that was sat in the centre of it.

It was an amusing enough story, but not one that piqued my interest in Russian fables, but that did not stop Mike from dropping in a reference or two whenever he could.

"She stitched us up! She handed us over to the Germans, not once, but twice! If we had any good sense, we would kill her now!"

"What are you going to use to do that? A sharpened stick?"

"How would you—"

Mike shot a look over at me, as if accusing me of speaking to her without his prior knowledge. The look he received back from me was the exact same that I was giving him.

"I didn't say anything," he almost pleaded with me.

"You better start talking, Suzanne. Otherwise, there's going to be quite a lot of trouble heading our way."

She seemed reluctant to talk at first, as if she

suddenly realised that she had been caught out. I noticed her eyes quickly dart towards the door. She stayed where she was. Clever woman. There was no way that she would get very far, not with an incensed Mike on her heels.

"I know someone. A German soldier. He keeps me informed of these things. They're rumours and whispers mainly. But every now and then you know what he says is true."

"How?"

"You can see it in their eyes. They aren't just individual soldiers when they are here. They are a group. Everything that happens affects them together.

"They found the body of the soldier, with a stick in his neck. A dog apparently found him. Was going berserk and barking at the German as if he was waiting for his stick to be thrown."

I felt Mike glance over at me, but I did nothing but blink as I held my gaze on Suzanne.

"They are all scared at the moment. They know that there is something going on. But they don't have enough information to shut it all down."

"Where do they think they are getting all this information from?"

"I…I don't know. I have never asked him."

"You need to put a stop to it," Mike said, all of a sudden becoming quite defensive over the woman who, five minutes ago, he would have happily beaten to death.

His thinking was the same as mine. Suzanne had

been careless, foolish. The German soldier, whoever he was, knew that Suzanne was involved with us, and so by association, knew that she was implicit in the killing of the German soldier.

"Does he know where you live?"

"N-No, I do not think so. Do you think I am in danger?"

"Have they started searching for the killers yet?"

"No, not exactly. They are trying to keep things hidden, for now. They say they are looking for spies. It gives them the chance to search the houses without anyone really knowing what is going on."

There was a silence for a moment, an uneasy one, in which Alfred took his leave, presuming that we could all do with a cup of tea right now. He wasn't far wrong.

"What does this soldier get in return? Are you telling him about what you are doing?"

Her face flushed a bright red. "We are friends. But, occasionally, I do let slip about what is happening. It makes it seem more reciprocal. That way I know he won't just stop telling me these things."

"Did you tell him about us? The house search at Monsieur Plantier's house. Was that you?"

She shifted in her seat.

"You have to understand that I had to give him something that was worth more than just a rumour. He needed concrete evidence that I was a part of this movement. Besides, I needed to check that you were who you said you were."

"What's that supposed to mean?"

"There are stories of the Gestapo sending in spies like you. Then, when the network is slowly revealed, they are shut down, one by one. Arrests, executions and everything in between."

"But you saw us land in that field. You saw us come from that plane."

"That means nothing nowadays. The Germans are very inventive in trying to fool us. I needed to see if they would come after you. If they didn't, then I would know that you weren't who you claimed to be. If they did, then I would be able to trust you."

"They jolly well did come after us! And they damn well nearly killed us too! What would you have done if they had killed us? You would have lost two agents in the process!"

Mike was furious, his eyes, bulging as they had done in the forest, seemed to burn a ferocious red colour, as if he had been overcome by some sort of demonic influence.

"That was all part of the risk. Anyway, you made it out alive."

"Yes, with no thanks to you."

The tension continued to simmer away at the surface, as Alfred stumbled his way into the room with a tray of refreshments. I guessed it was half-time. The second half would kick off again soon.

Mike's eyes seemed intent on burning a hole in Suzanne's forehead, causing her to stand from her chair and walk over to the window, staring up and down the street outside, searching for the truck that had trundled past moments ago.

I had nowhere else to look, so found myself staring at the portrait above the fireplace, for what felt like the thousandth time. The picture was as entertaining as anything that I had seen before, each and every time I looked at it, I noticed something new. A new crease in his face, a new blemish, each one appearing as if the picture was somehow ageing alongside my own face.

"Alfred," I croaked, forcing a sip of tea down my throat, which was somehow only lukewarm. "That boy, in the picture. Who is he?"

The old man looked straight into my eyes, as he lowered himself into his chair, gingerly. His arms seemed stiff as he withdrew his handkerchief and delicately dabbed his nose with it, the red embroidery flashing around the room as he did so. He had never struck me as the kind of man to move around the room in pain, so why he had cautiously lowered his body into the chair was beyond me.

"That…that is my son."

"Yes, and we don't talk about him. Do we Alfred?"

The old man, as petrified of the young woman as ever, shook his head in agreement with her.

22

It would be easier for me to keep the whole thing quiet, never to be mentioned again, than it would be for Mike. He had only lasted a couple of months before blurting out the truth about what had happened to Teddy Higgins, whereas I was still able to keep a lid on the truth as I sat, still staring at the portrait of the young man.

The lid, that had stayed firmly in its place for the best part of a year now, had begun to wobble in the last couple of days. It had almost slipped from its place completely at Suzanne's outburst towards Alfred. But still, I managed to keep it on, at least to the outside world anyway, not one of the others knew what was tumbling through my mind, as I sat there catatonic for what must have been an hour or two.

I looked towards Mike, as I had done on *that* night, the same expression that he had had on his face then, slowly morphing its way onto his face in Alfred's house. We were not there, of course we weren't, but for a moment or two, I could not distinguish between what was real, and what was playing itself over in my head.

"Can you lads help us anymore?" an elderly gentleman, steel helmet pulled over to one side, called out to us as he stumbled his way through the loose bricks and debris.

"Really sorry, old chap. But we must be heading off now. Our CO will be wondering where it is we have got to."

The man's face fell, momentarily, as if he understood that we must do our duty, but also disappointed that the two strong, well-fed chaps in front of him were no longer at his disposal.

Regardless, even if we could have helped them out, it did not mean that I would have done. I had already seen enough. I knew London was getting it bad, but I didn't want to have to be the one that was dealing with it head-on. I was perfectly alright with going head to head with the bombers, angels two-zero, where all that could kill me were the rounds that zipped from the end of an MG15.

At least, in the air, the only person that I could blame for my death would be myself. It would be a mistake that I had made that would kill me.

On the ground, as the bombs fell all around you, it was the luck of the draw. As if some mythical giant had dropped a handful of conkers, the unfortunate few who lay in its path with nothing to protect them other than a thin layer of concrete at best.

"That's a shame chaps. We are really taking a hammering tonight. Two waves already, and it's not even eleven o'clock yet. The south-west Londoners are taking a few hits as well, from what I've heard."

My interest was inextinguishable, and I could almost feel the sigh from Mike as he realised that I would now no longer be returning with him, even if he managed to carry me onto the train.

"Where abouts in the south-west?" I asked, tentatively, not really wanting to know what was happening down there.

"All of them. Twickenham, Putney, Kew."

"And Richmond?"

"I daresay they've taken a few, Sir. Although we ain't heard much from their brigade down there, truth be told."

I looked to Mike.

"I've got to go there, Mike," I could already feel the whimpering tears threatening to roll down my cheeks. I made sure that they stayed in there for now. I could not crumble at this point.

"I know you do, old fruit. Come on, I'll come with you."

I didn't offer up any kind of argument or protests as, in truth, it felt good that he was coming with me. I wouldn't have thought any less of him if he had decided that it was not for him, it was not his family after all, but the fact that he was prepared to come meant the world to me.

It took us a good ninety minutes to make the journey across London to Richmond, having to apologetically turn down hundreds of pleas for help as we did so. Some cabbies were still running defiantly, not even allowing the falling bombs to stop them from picking up a passenger or two.

"The gits tried to stop me with shells twenty years ago lads. They failed then. They'll fail again tonight. Put it away son," he finished off, as I went to pass him a handful of coins.

"Only the desperate are out looking for cabs tonight. And I make sure not to take a fare off anyone who is that desperate. I hope you find your family."

"Thank you," I gasped, as I was already hurdling over smashed walls and broken windows, running through the town to the place where I had, until recently, lived happily with my family.

I charged past the town square, which had over the previous couple of months, been a hotbed of local activity, as money was raised for a fighter plane.

There had been all sorts of goings-on in the locality to raise funds for what became known as The Jubilee Fighter, including showing bits of a smashed Dornier that had been shot down somewhere over central London. There were tales of schoolchildren raiding piggy banks and downright thievery, all the way to the tramp who had managed to scrape together three farthings for the cause.

"It is all that I can muster," had been his remorseful sigh to the shop owner.

But now, the joviality and fun of fundraising was nothing but a ghost in the square, as bits of broken water fountain lay strewn across my path. I leapt over it athletically, and seconds later I heard Mike do the same until we came screeching to a halt, at the top of Sheen Road, which had become a hubbub of activity.

"You can't go down there, Sir," a plump faced, sixty-something man said as he stepped across my path. "Who are you?"

"Flying Officer Johnny Parker. And who are you?"

"Captain Derwin, 2nd Platoon, Richmond Home Guard. We're overseeing the rescue efforts here."

"Rescue efforts?"

"Can't you see, Sir? We've been bombed. Mightily hard at that. This road here has had all its houses destroyed."

"This is Peldon Avenue?"

"Well…it *was* Peldon Avenue, Sir. You know this area well?"

I did not wait around to give him an answer, and I heard Mike give the bloke a good shove behind me.

"We're coming through, he lives here!"

I could not tell where it was number thirty-two had once stood, but I stopped in the middle of the street and looked around me. To my surprise, there were no armed men giving chase to the two who had just barged through the perimeter, just sad and confused faces as they wondered where to begin.

"W-What happened?"

"Parachute mines, Sir."

"Did they all detonate?"

"As far as we know, Sir."

I had heard of parachute mines before, although I had never seen the scale of devastation with which they truly operated. They would fall from the aircraft, immediately opening up a parachute and would dangle their way to earth, in a similar fashion to a pilot who had baled out of his aircraft.

They would then descend comparatively slowly to a normal bomb, before detonating some fifty feet from the ground, the idea being that the blast of the bomb would be far more effective, without the obstacles around it to absorb the blast.

I had no idea how many had fallen on Peldon Avenue, but they had done their job. The entire street had been reduced to a pile of rubble and broken glass.

"Well, come on then! Let's get a move on!" Another man appeared at the end of the street, with a tin hat on, just like most of the others around there, with 'POLICE' stencilled in white on the front.

He didn't look like a police officer, nor did he speak like one, as he began to boss people around with language that would have made even a deaf man blush awfully.

The rest of the men around us sprang into action, with a terrific efficiency, moving piles of brick around and fallen door frames, collecting them in the middle of the street where they were confident that no one could be buried.

Within seconds, my hands were a mess of blisters and pockmarked with blood, as I ignored the shards of glass that had begun to protrude from them. There was far more at risk here than a few surface wounds.

"Over here!" someone screamed, with such an urgency that I felt the vocal cords begin to strain under the pressure. "There's a baby here!"

I felt my heart stop dead as he looked over at me. There was something behind his eyes that told me that he knew who I was. My whole body flushed with a chill as I made my way over to him.

There were plenty of others already there by the time I got to him, but for all I cared, it could have just been me and the baby.

"Come on, Johnny, let's get you out of here. You don't need to see this," Mike tugged at my shoulder, compassionately.

"No!" I found myself screaming as the dirt rolled down my cheeks, beaten away by the tears. I felt a surge of bile and vomit burning at the back of my throat and nose, but I somehow managed to keep it down long enough to utter a few more words.

"That's my son. That's my boy…"

The pain in my knees, as I stumbled over an old dining room table, connecting with the bricks that surrounded me, didn't seem to register. Not above the amount of pain that was coursing through my heart anyway.

The people all around me parted, compassionately, as one or two helped the quivering wreck to be reunited with his son.

Henry's eyes were closed. Which was a merciful blessing, as I stared at him. He looked as though he was asleep. I spoke to him gently, as if he was snoozing and that I could wake him up at any moment.

Grace had always told me off about that. Even when I had not seen him in a number of weeks, she resented the fact that I would pick him up from his basket, no matter the time of day or night, and cradle and talk to him as if he was wide awake. Inevitably, he would wake, and scream and shout at the top of his little lungs when he did so.

And I loved every second of it.

"I'm sorry, my little man. I'm so sorry."

But now, no matter how hard or loudly I talked, there was nothing that I could do to wake him. There was nothing that I could do to protect him.

My tears splashed on his perfect little face, all his features barely formed, completely unblemished by the pains of the world, now frozen in time.

"Come on, old fruit. Let's get you both out of here."

I looked up at Mike, my eyes in almost as much agony as my heart.

"My boy. My little boy."

"I know, old fruit. I know."

"What about Grace?"

"They'll find her soon enough. I'm sure she's fine. Let's just get you and Henry somewhere safe, shall we?"

Through my grief, I almost didn't hear the shouts of "UXB!" but still, they somehow managed to permeate into my consciousness, as they rippled down the street.

"UXB!"

"We've got a UXB over 'ere."

"Let the BD boys know they're needed in Peldon Avenue!"

I thought it odd, as I turned around to face the young boy who had found Henry, that he had somehow managed to find my son, before he spotted the large German bomb. But finding Henry he had, which I put down to some sort of divine providence, that I managed to spend a few moments with my son before the whole street was closed down by the Bomb Disposal boys.

But the BD boys needn't have bothered making their way to Richmond that night. They were only needed for a brief window of ten to fifteen seconds. After that, it had been pointless.

The first thing that I knew about it, was feeling the excruciating heat on my right arm as I turned. After that, everything else had gone black.

23

"Do you want to talk about it?"

"About what?"

"Whatever it is that has been occupying your mind since we left Alfred's house."

I looked across at her. Her eyes did not seem at all interesting, there was nothing really to note about them, but she somehow had the ability to command my entire attention with them. I wondered whether that was how she had got her German to confide in her or if she had some other hypnotic powers to do the heavy lifting.

"That depends," I said, my eyes scanning over her freckles, joining them up like a dot-to-dot.

"On what?"

I thought for a moment, wondering whether or not this was a good game to be playing with a woman like her. I still did not know if I could trust her, despite the innocent twinkle in her eye, and the plumpness to her skin similar to that of a child's.

As I continued to stare at her face, I wondered how on earth she could have possibly been some sort of double agent. She just didn't seem to have it in her. But, then again, she was out in the forest with us, preparing to execute our mission which, judging by her face at least, didn't seem part of her repertoire.

But, then again, maybe that was what made her such a good fighter. She didn't look like one. It was probably how she had managed to gain the German's trust.

We had told her that now was the best time to break it off with her German friend. Security was paramount to us, and we could not verify how secure her friendship was, especially as we could not guarantee what kind of information she was giving back the other way.

If Mike and I were to survive there, in the long-term, we would need to establish our own network, our own intelligence sources. Which meant severing the ones that already existed. I wondered if she knew yet what that meant for her German friend. There had been no hint in her eyes that she knew we would have to kill him.

He knew too much and, if he had not done so already, would eventually hand Suzanne over to the authorities the minute he guessed that she was no longer playing his game. So, we had to get to him first. But we would have to deal with that later, there were more urgent things in the mix at the moment. Like our *Genrealfeldmarschall.*

"It depends on whether you start talking to me."

"I have spoken to you."

"You know what I mean. I want to know what you are hiding from us. We are here to help you, not hinder us. To be able to do that, we need to know everything."

"I have told you everything!" she protested with vigour.

Mike glanced backwards towards us angrily, from his hide that he had created out of more twigs and stones. There was no sharpened branch this time, but an MP40, a German submachine gun that one of Suzanne's helpers had somehow managed to accumulate.

Mike was nervous, not just about the operation, but about the weapon he had been given. The MP40 was as smooth as butter to fire, quite as if it wasn't a gun at all, but a paintbrush, when it felt like firing that was. It had a tendency to jam, and we had spent many hours up in the Highlands of Scotland, deliberately jamming and unjamming the gun to get used to the way it worked.

It was the first time that Mike had operated one under pressure before, and that's where things always went wrong.

We got the message from his glare and made sure to lower our voices as we camped out in the bushes. There were about fifteen of us, all told, hidden alongside the same stretch of road that Mike and I had hidden in a few days' before.

In fact, it would take us less than two minutes to find the unfortunate German's body, somewhere over to my left.

"You know what I mean, Suzanne. You've been so obsessed with who *we* are, that you've barely told us a thing about yourself. Every time we've tried to poke into your life, the shutters have come down. You ran away to the north. Then you came back, why was that? Why does Alfred seem so scared of you? Monsieur Plantier too."

"I do not know why they are scared of me. Perhaps it is because they have made one mistake too many. I do not like mistakes. If people keep making them, they're out. I no longer use them. I am not as unconcerned by security as you seem to think."

"Fair enough."

She gave a sigh, as if what she was about to tell me was not entirely voluntary, but that she had grown tired of hiding it any longer.

"I have told no one this," she began, looking around as if someone might be listening in. There was nobody with us, except for one disgruntled Brit and twelve other Frenchmen.

"Madame Soyer was English. I, of course, had known her for a very long time."

She looked at me as if to say that I should have known exactly who Madame Soyer was and that the confused look on my face was completely unwarranted.

She rolled onto her side for a moment, withdrawing a twig that was embedding itself into her belly, before tossing it over her shoulder. I had already grown used to the discomfort that we would inevitably be in for the next few hours, but figured that it would take Suzanne a little while longer before she gave up.

“Madame Soyer…Elizabeth Soyer was a well-connected and well-known English woman. She came to France some years ago with her family, to meet the man that she was betrothed to be married to. Some sort of a business arrangement,” she added, flitting her hand away as if none of it really mattered anymore.

“But there was a scandal. She ran away, with another man. He was the footman to her father while he was here in France. She lost everything; her family, her home, her inheritance. She married someone else.”

“A Frenchman?”

“You really have no idea who it is, do you?”

“Am I meant to?”

“Monsieur Soyer…Alfred Soyer.”

“Alfred was the footman?”

“He lost everything too. His family disowned him. He lost his livelihood. No one would employ him after what had happened. But they did it all in the name of love.”

“And they all lived happily ever after?”

The sarcasm, as ever, sailed high over her head. I made a mental note to simply stop with the quips, as I was getting nowhere with her.

"No. They did, for a while, I suppose. Until they had a child. A son. But they could not afford to live any longer. So, they decided that Elizabeth and Charles should go back to England. To plead with her family for support and send him to school there. Since then, Alfred has not seen either of them."

I stopped her for a moment, as Mike signalled to us that he had heard something. To begin with, I struggled to hear anything that resembled a threat, apart from a pair of flapping wings as a bird hunted down its dinner for the evening.

But then, just above the flapping wings, I heard something odd. Mike had very good ears to have heard that sort of thing from such a distance.

But quickly, the higher-pitched drone of an aircraft engine came within earshot, and everyone was silent, holding their breath in for as long as possible.

Then, as if it was following the road for some sort of bearing, a *Fieseler Fi* 156 came into view. It was a flimsy-looking aircraft, almost like a child's toy, where everything seemed to be made out of the most vulnerable of materials possible.

But it had an excellent engine, which meant that it could take off in such a short area, that it could find a clearing anywhere it liked and, at that moment, my thoughts were obsessed with trying to recall if we had seen one in the middle of the forest somewhere.

Our main concern, however, as it slowly trundled past, at almost eye-level, was that it was looking for something, or more worryingly, someone.

Within a matter of seconds, I heard the pitch of the engine change, as the pilot throttled forwards, and put the aircraft into a steep climb, banking away to the west to chase the setting sun.

"Did he see us?" I rasped, in Mike's direction.

"Not sure, but we'll find out soon enough."

The engine throbbed off into the distance, and for the time being, we were safe. At least he wasn't coming back around for a second glance.

"How do you know so much?" I asked Suzanne, who had obviously thought that her story-telling time was up.

"About what?"

"About Alfred and his family."

She mumbled apologetically, as she tried to get comfortable for a second time.

"Madame Soyer and I wrote to each other quite frequently. Until about October '39. She was worried about the war, worried about Alfred. But more urgently, she was worried about her son."

"Why?"

"He had joined your air force and was sent to France as part of the Advanced Air Striking Force. He was one of the first British servicemen to get here. So, I went up to *Mourmelon* to find him. I figured that if I could turn his head, keep him focused, then he would get home to his mother and father after the war."

"What happened?"

"It didn't go to plan."

"In what way?"

"We fell in love. Got married. No one was particularly approving of it. Not least the Group Captain who Charles had to get permission from. It was all rather frowned upon."

There was a silence, that lingered a little too long for my liking, it had not taken me long to process the fact that Suzanne was Alfred's daughter-in-law. I did not know how long we were going to be laying there for, but it could be as little as sixty seconds, and I wanted as much information from her as I could.

"What happened to him?"

She looked at me, frustrated, as if I hadn't had to ask such a foolish question. I already knew the answer.

"He was killed. May 1940. He was flying Fairey Battles, shot down as the Germans advanced. Died in the crash, apparently."

"I'm sorry."

I couldn't fake my remorse that her husband had been killed. I had known many good pilots to die in much the same way, not that she knew that. But there was a twinge in my soul each and every time that I heard another pilot had gone down, on either side. I knew what it felt like, to feel all-powerful, up there in the sky, only to be told otherwise by a short cannon-burst, which for some would be the last thing that they ever heard.

"It's funny," she continued, quite voluntarily this time. "Do you know what their squadron motto was?"

I shook my head.

"*En garde.* That always tickled us both for some reason."

En Garde. En Garde. I had seen that squadron motto printed somewhere but struggled to recall where I had seen it.

But then, as I strained to conjure up where I had seen it, it began to come to me. The crest, in the same shape as all the other squadron crests, had a serpent, tangling its way through the middle, its forked tongue out and ready to strike.

En Garde ran along the bottom.

"Eighty-eight Squadron."

Her head flicked around, so fast that I feared she may have done herself some damage in the process.

"How would you know that?" she spat, accusingly, as if I had just made her spit out all of her history completely needlessly.

I smiled weakly, to try to ease the tension somewhat.

"I've seen the squadron crest. In a pub, near Boscombe Down…the photo, the one on Alfred's fireplace, is that Charles?"

She nodded, tearfully.

"I've seen it before. Only in uniform. What rank was he?"

"Squadron Leader. Squadron Leader Talbot. He

took his mother's maiden name when he moved back to England."

"Squadron Leader Talbot. I'll have a drink for him next time I'm in that pub. Maybe one day you could join me."

"I would like that very much."

She shuffled over again, brushing a series of ants from her stomach and insisting that she be made as comfortable as she could.

I suddenly felt quite warm, as if I had opened up a new side to her, one that she had kept hidden for many years. There was even a chance that we could start to trust each other soon.

But I wasn't going to count my chickens just yet.

24

I sat in a contented silence, for some time, just allowing the final few rays of sunshine to warm my skin, before they retired for the evening. For the first time since I had arrived in France, I found myself to be quite contented, relaxed almost. A few more days of this and I could be classed as someone who was, in fact, enjoying themselves.

Mike, however, was not. He fidgeted and rustled around behind the barricade of branches that he had made for himself, as he fretted over the positions and hiding places of the Frenchmen that were laying alongside us.

I could see, in the way that his body moved, all tense and rigid, that he was concerned. Our plan was to wait for a vehicle to come along, any vehicle, before we acted but, so far, the only one that we had seen in the five hours that we had been there was one that was a hundred feet from the ground.

For our plan to work, we needed something firmly on the ground. Preferably with tyres.

My body ached and groaned as I slowly leant on either side of my hips, allowing a rush of blood to fill the void that had been denied any real sustenance for hours. We were getting closer to when we expected it all to kick off, and I needed to be ready for what was about to happen.

At the thought of what might happen, I pulled the old revolver out of the waistband of my trousers, that I had tucked away a couple of hours ago. It was impractical to have it in my palm the whole time while I was laying on the floor, but I wanted to have it touching a part of my body at all times, for fear of what might happen if I lost it.

It was an 1892 revolver, which had seen plenty of action in the last war amongst the French officers. Where Suzanne and her team had managed to find this one was beyond me, but it seemed well maintained enough to still work when I pulled the trigger.

It was small, moulded well enough to look almost pretty in one's grip, but the front seemed far heavier than I had expected, which gave it an almost downward trajectory the moment you lifted it up to fire. It was either that, or it had been so long since I had handled a weapon, that I had forgotten what it felt like.

According to Alfred, the gun was produced mainly with French cavalrymen in mind, the cylinder swinging out to the right to reload, rather than the left, so that a man on horseback would be able to reload with his dominant hand.

It was a handy feature, for the cavalryman. But it made it awkward and cumbersome to reload for someone who was not on horseback. Someone like me.

Nevertheless, Alfred had taken great pleasure in showing me the basics of the revolver, prompting me to ask the inevitable question of how he knew so much.

"This continent has been at war for centuries, Jean. Every man for generations has been taught how to kill another, in the easiest way possible."

I talked myself through the process that Alfred had shown me; pulling back on the loading gate and swinging the cylinder out and over to the right-hand side. Inside, as there had been for the last few hours, were six eight-millimetre cartridges, all brightly glinting in the fading light of the day.

I clicked the cylinder back into place but kept the loading gate where it was. Having it pulled backwards meant that the hammer was disengaged, which prevented me from accidentally putting a round into my own backside, while I was laying in the forest.

It might have worked back in Alfred's day, but shooting myself was not going to get me sent home. If anything, it was likely to prevent me from getting back home one day.

It was the first time that I had ever really thought of home. I felt like I had nowhere to go now, after I had lost everything, but as I sat in that forest, waiting for whatever it was to come down the road, I realised that maybe, part of me did want to make it out of this alive, and that everything was not lost.

"A penny for your thoughts."

I looked over at Suzanne, whose face had seemed to grow a little softer in the last hour or so, as if she was somehow warming to the idea that two British men could, in fact, be helpful to her.

"Sorry," she muttered, with a slight chuckle, "It was always one of Charles' favourite sayings. He always said that I was locked in my own world."

I smiled back at her, softly, before turning to look back down towards the road that had become so ingrained in my eyes that I began to see it everywhere I looked.

"Anyway, a penny for them?"

I had nothing to lose by telling her. Besides, she had confided in me, it was about time that I repaid some of that trust.

"I'm just thinking of home. I haven't really let myself since I've been here."

"Why not?"

"Too distracting. I want to focus on what I'm meant to be doing here."

A bunch of flies began to want to use my face as a landing strip, as they fluttered around my mouth and nose, and more than one was sucked up and into my lungs. I flapped them away gently, not wanting to cause so much of a raucous that we would compromise ourselves. Everyone else was having to deal with it, so I should suffer with them.

"But it is good to have something to focus on. A reward for doing what you're doing."

"And what's your reward?"

She exhaled out of her nose sharply, and I couldn't work out if it was because she was laughing at me, or simply trying to get rid of the pesky flies under her nostrils.

"I would suppose that mine is very different to yours and Monsieur Houdin," she changed her gaze, to look over towards Mike, and I wondered whether she was half-hoping that he would be listening in. But I didn't think Mike could hear either of us, over the tension and rigidity that had taken over his whole being.

"You and Michel are here because this is where you have been told to go. Your way of fighting is one of self-preservation. You want to do each mission as it comes, get through it, in the hope that one day you can see home again. You want to live. Am I right so far?"

"Yes, quite…But you're not like that?"

"This is my country, Jean. There are people here running it now that would have no qualms in shooting us in the head if we looked at them the wrong way. They treat us as if we are dogs. We need them to be gone.

"They have taken everything from me. I want to make their lives as uncomfortable as possible here. I want them to be looking over their shoulders all the time. I will not rest until they are either out of my country, or I am dead. Do you understand?"

I understood perfectly but couldn't quite shake the feeling that I had somehow just been given a dressing down. Her eyes were ablaze with passion as she spoke, and for the first time, I could see what it was that made so many men completely terrified of her.

She seemed to believe every word that she was saying. It was either that or she was the best liar that I had ever come across. Deep down, I wanted to believe her, to trust her more, but there was an element to it all which seemed fabricated, an alarm bell somewhere in my mind. I wanted to believe her, to trust her, but I simply couldn't. Not that easily anyway.

She seemed to calm down hugely over the next twenty seconds or so.

"So, do you have a family waiting for you back at home?"

"Well…" I started, unable to really finish off the rest of the sentence.

The obvious answer would be that I *had* a family. But the more complex, and troubling answer would be to the question that would inevitably follow.

What happened to them?

They died in a bombing raid in London almost a year before. Both of them. My new-born son and my wife. But it didn't have to be like that.

In my mind, they were far away from London, in Norfolk, where they filled their days with trips to the coast or on the canals. Henry would be learning to walk around about now, and I would be excited to get back home to see him again.

But, in reality, none of that could happen. The chance to go to Norfolk, to live with Grace's parents, had been rejected. Not because Grace hadn't wanted to go, but on my own, foolish insistence.

"They wouldn't dare to bomb London," had been on everyone's lips at the beginning of the war, and the ferocity with which I had battled with German bombers over the south of England persuaded me that they would never really get close.

I had wanted them to stay in London, so that it would have been easier for me to see them when I was stationed at Weald. The thought of them being several hours away in Norfolk saddened me to my soul.

But then, the unthinkable began to happen; bombs fell on London. And they kept coming.

But, by then it was too late. My insistence had seeped into Grace's determination.

No one else was running away to the country, so why should she?

An Anderson shelter would suffice. Besides, we lived in Richmond, what was there to bomb anyway?

I opened my mouth to speak but no words came out at first. Just a low growl.

I stopped myself from saying anything further, as I caught Mike's eye as he turned to look at me. He wasn't best pleased with the noises that I was making.

I closed my jaw and looked down at the pile of dried leaves in front of me.

But the noise kept coming.

Suzanne began to shuffle around, drawing her weapon, a farmer's shotgun, up to her face.

Mike's eyes were suddenly filled with jubilation and relief, as if this encounter with the enemy was all that he had been waiting for, his entire life.

I squinted down towards the road, to see if I could make out the contraptions that we had laid down earlier on.

Somewhere, down in the dusky darkness, the kind that could only come in the middle of a forest, were a series of spikes, embedded into the ground.

Caltrops, to be precise. They were medieval-looking things, which was probably down to the fact that they had been used since the middle ages. Historically, the sharp metal would be buried into the ground, in the hope of stopping everything from foot soldiers, all the way up to the armoured vehicles of the day; war elephants.

I winced at the terrible howls the magnificent beast would make as the poor thing trod on one of the sharpened spikes, sending its riders in a plethora of directions as it tried to shake them off. The thunder that would rumble around the ground as the stricken animal fell would be akin to an artillery shell exploding right beside you.

But, that night, our target was not an elephant

laden with explosives and soldiers. It was any kind of vehicle that we could lay our hands-on.

We had buried five in the ground, on the approach road to the *Château de Serrane*. They zig-zagged across the path of any vehicle in the hope that we would catch at least one tyre and render the vehicle useless.

As the motorcycle came sweeping around the corner, from the direction of the town, the purr of its engine began to develop nicely in my ears.

We were doing this with a handicap; we did not know if and when the *Gernealfeldmarschall* would return to the Château, but we assumed that he would do so around nightfall, in time for some supper before bed.

The single torch beam of the motorcycle's head-light bobbed its way down the centre of the road, the top half taped off slightly so that only a narrow beam could bounce on the track.

Then, just above the noise of its revving engine, a voice.

"He's missed the first one."

"And the second."

I held my breath. If he missed them all, then we could be in for a very long night.

But then there was the sudden sound of screaming. Not from a human, or even an animal, but the scream of metal as it ground its way along the road. The engine revved incredibly high, bellowing louder than the shriek of metal on gravel.

The narrowed headlight spun around on the floor

erratically, before coming to a stop. Then there was a silence.

We waited for a moment, to make sure that no one was coming up behind him that would take all of us by surprise.

But there was nothing.

By the time that the rider had seen the caltrop, if at all, it had been far too late for him.

Before I could so much as pull myself to my feet, there were already four Frenchmen surrounding the body, that had curled himself up tightly in a ball.

This was where it all started. This was what I was enjoying.

25

By the time that I had made it to the fallen motorcyclist, he was already being dragged across the road, to the ditch where some of the Frenchmen had been laying in wait.

It must have been pretty obvious to the German that we had been there for some time, as the eagerness with which he was being tugged across the road was with a force the likes of which I had never seen before.

As they pulled him, he tried his best to find his feet, leaving great scuff marks from one side of the road to the other. Mike hastily retraced the two odd gauges in the dusty track, scuffing back over them to make sure that no one could guess at what they were.

The man was quickly separated from various parts of his uniform, as a few others went and recovered the motorcycle that was resting some ten yards away from where he had fallen, the wheels still spinning gently.

It was a useless trophy for us. There was no way that anyone could make any use of it. If they did, it would only act as a roaring beacon to the Germans over who had carried out the attack, and it wasn't the kind of vehicle that one could take to the butchers, without turning a few heads.

The leather satchel that was dangling around his waist was quickly whipped over his head, the contents of which was thumbed through vigorously, as if they expected to find something of great importance within it. But their search was fruitless.

The MP40 that was tethered over his neck, and had been resting on his lap, was too taken from him, his eyes filled with sadness at the thought that, as a soldier, he was now practically naked.

Everything was taken from him, including his helmet and dust goggles, which were hastily thrown over to me. I inspected them for a moment, running my hand around the inside of the helmet, trying to judge if it would be a good fit or not.

As the motorcycle was wheeled towards me, I recognised it as the BMW R12, the same ones that I had seen plenty of back in *Tours*, with the number plate glued onto the front wheel arch precariously.

It was a drab grey colour, as if somehow the machine was incredibly sad, and had wanted nothing more than to be crashed in the way she had been. The engine, beneath the rider, was exposed, which was why it made the most terrific purring noise as it trundled along.

The two side saddle metal boxes, on both the left and right, were rifled through in much the same way as the leather satchel, as files and pieces of paper were quickly read, before being passed onto someone else.

"*Bitte...*" the man began, as he realised that he was going to be in a fight for his life here. His eyes were forlorn and submissive, not wanting to look at anyone for too long. He looked around at us quickly, locking his eyes onto me. I must have had the kindest looking face. Or maybe it was just the fear that he could sense in me.

"*Bitte...Ich habe eine Familie...Bitte...*"

I spoke a little German, not much, but enough to know that what he was saying was the usual drivel that our instructors had used back when we were training in the Highlands.

Please, I have a family.

It was the kind of tosh that anyone would try on their captors, even if it wasn't true. And if I had been taught anything during my training for this work, then it was that the Germans would do and say anything to try and get out alive.

His gaze on me held firm, even as he was dragged towards the side of the road and up the bank. Scrabbling together, with a pair of hands under each armpit, the German knew that he was in trouble. He needed to get away from us in the next sixty seconds, or he might not be getting away from us at all.

He began writhing around and struggling, like a recently caught fish that was doing all it could to get thrown back into the water. But he was having very little luck.

Eventually, he kicked out, catching one of the Frenchmen in the groin, which seemed to anger a lot more people than just his victim. Mike was one of those, incensed that he would have the audacity to try and take us all on, rather than curl up and take what was coming.

Mike stepped forward, his knuckles glowing white, and delivered a firm blow into the gut of the German, his leather jerkin being sucked into the vortex of air that it created. The German, grunting, doubled over in pain, with the Frenchmen who gripped able to do nothing to stop him.

Mike leant over him, "Now you are going to do as you're told. Got it?"

The German, to his credit, was not going to give up without a jolly good fight.

As he heard Mike's voice, he shot upwards, knowing full well where Mike's face would be. The back of his head connected wonderfully with Mike's face. I couldn't tell where, but to the German, none of that mattered. As long as he injured as many of us as possible, the finesse of his moves mattered not a jot.

Mike recoiled from the German, clutching at his face somewhere, as Suzanne appeared in front of him. I could tell that he was already experiencing the headache as a result of his assault on Mike, but at that moment, his biggest headache was going to be the small, but towering, figure of the Frenchwoman that now stood in front of him.

She took a step backwards, as if inspecting his face, but in reality just guarding herself from the same sort of fate that had just come upon Mike, who was still clutching at his face.

Using the back of her hand, she delivered one of the most vicious slaps that I had ever seen in my life. The German simply stared back at her, defiantly, if not a little bit worried that he was being punished as a child would be.

"*Der Generalfeldmarschall. Er ist heute Nacht hier?*"

Her German sounded inch-perfect to me, almost as good as her English had been. Even Mike, whose cheek was a sticky scarlet mess, looked up to me, concerned at her eloquence in the German tongue.

The German, whose earlier courage and determination had waned considerably quickly, refused to answer.

She repeated herself.

The Generalfeldmarschall. He is here tonight?

Still, nothing.

"*Deine Familie. Du willst sie wiedersehen? Sprechen.*"

To the German's credit, it did not seem like he had lied earlier on, as Suzanne's little threat, spat through gritted teeth, had had the desired effect.

Your family. You want to see them again? Speak.

"*Dreiundzwanzig Uhr. Er kehrt vom Abendessen zurück.*"

"What is he saying?" Mike said, his tongue sounding ever so swollen.

I went to tell him, but Suzanne got there first.

"He is due to return at eleven this evening. He has been out to dinner."

Suzanne continued to talk to him, while I looked back at Mike.

"You alright, mate?"

He looked at me, furious that I had even asked.

"Little swine made me bleed," he muttered, his pride in tatters. "If she hadn't stepped in, I would have killed him."

"Oh yeah," I said with a smile, "You really looked like threatening him from where I was standing."

"Leave off, will you."

Suzanne backed away from the German and made her way over to us. I sensed that we had all the information that we needed from the motorcycle rider, and that now was the time that the real work began.

"Hide that bike in the bushes somewhere!" I called out to the three men who stood around it, marvelling at the engineering work and wondering how they were going to restore it back to working order. "And make sure that you can't see it from the road! If you can see it, so will they."

Spinning around, I urgently called out to all the others, who had been nothing more than bystanders in the whole affair.

"Back up the hill. The lot of you wait there for us."

I checked my wristwatch, as Suzanne and Mike, who had managed to stem the blood flow down his cheek, came over to join me, in the middle of the road. It was just before ten o'clock. We still had a reasonably long wait ahead of us. But that was fine.

It meant that we could now come up with a plan, and then run through everything in our heads, to work out where it might falter.

I stared down at the caltrop that the motorcyclist had struck, one prong driven into the ground with three more, sharpened edges, protruding in three different directions. One towards the house, another southwards back down the track towards the town and one final one, pointing straight up to the heavens.

Judging by the way that one of them was all bent out of shape, I guessed that the motorcycle had struck the one that was pointing back towards the town, and that he had been going at some speed to have bent it.

"That's that one finished with," I said, bending down to inspect the broken rod.

"What rot," Mike said, his bloodied face joining mine down by the caltrop. "That could still take out a tank, that could. Besides, there are four others that he could still hit."

"You aren't considering still using these things for Sperrle are you?" Suzanne asked, her thin frame towering over the two crouching Brits. In unison, we stood up to meet her, just as I realised that my legs were a mix of burning fire and dilapidated old trunks.

"Of course," Mike answered, indignantly. We had trained for months for this sort of thing, and he seemed mightily offended that someone else, with no training, was about to offer an alternative to our way of thinking.

"Well," I conceded, "That depends on what you make of the situation."

She yanked the old rifle onto her shoulder, pulling out a packet of cigarettes. She offered neither of us one, as I watched Mike's eyes trace her every move, before sucking in some of the smoke that she had ejected.

"Men like Sperrle don't drive around in one car. They always have at least an outrider. Maybe even a second car. If they see the motorcycles ahead of them go down. They'll know something is up immediately. All they will have to do is back up, and your man will be in the wind."

I hated to admit it, especially as I could not be quite sure on whose side she was on, but the logic was sound enough.

"What we need to do, is bring the whole convoy to a halt, regardless of how many vehicles there are. That way, we will be able to identify which one is Sperrle and deal with him accordingly. It gives you more of a chance of stopping all of them, without them becoming too suspicious. It also increases your chances of actually getting anywhere near Sperrle."

I looked at Mike, who seemed far more concerned with the state of his face than with what Suzanne was suggesting. He seemed completely disinterested.

"It sounds good to me," I said, looking over to Mike, whose interest had suddenly piqued.

"What? You can't be serious? Why wouldn't we go with what we've been trained to do?"

"Because," I snapped back, "Suzanne has been here before. What she has said makes sense."

"Ten minutes ago, she was telling the Germans who we were and where we were staying, and now you're trusting her like this?"

"As a matter of fact, yes I am. And if you don't like it, you can jolly well shoot me."

He stared me down for a moment, as I felt my face, flushed more than ever before, burn out of embarrassment, but also disappointment.

I couldn't quite believe that Mike and I had fallen out in the way that we had. I had not seen it coming, nor had he. But his temperament, blowing hot and cold; tense and fearful one moment, lacklustre and disinterested the next, had frustrated me a little too far.

He chewed on the inside of his damaged cheek, as if removing the final few specks of blood that had leaked into it, still holding onto my gaze. For a moment I truly thought that he was going to swing the submachine gun up and put a round or two into me.

"What's the plan then?" he asked, finally. Turning

his head over to Suzanne, who seemed mightily pleased that she had seemed to have won us round.

"Well, I've been giving it some thought. What do you reckon to this?"

As she took in another breath, I noticed that she was taking a long hard look at the German helmet and dust goggles that I was still clutching a hold to.

26

Mike chuckled and spluttered as he heard Suzanne's plan for me. He seemed to take great pleasure from watching my face morph into one of total fear and desperation.

"Sticking to our original plan doesn't seem so bad now, does it, old fruit?"

I gave him a sharp look, one that told him that he needed to be quiet immediately, or he could find himself with another gash on his face.

He looked down at his feet, smirking. It was fair enough; I would have been doing the exact same thing if it was him who was being touted as the bait in the trap.

Part of me did, in fact, wish that we had continued with the original plan. The caltrops were all still in place and would be a mighty effort of manpower to dig them out. We would then need to refill the holes, covering them up enough so that, to the naked eye, they didn't look as if they had recently been dug over.

It also meant that everyone had been briefed on the same plan, not the one that we were going to have to come up with on the spot. I made a mental note to make sure that every man knew of the change in circumstances, otherwise, there was a very real threat that I could end up dead as the result of another man's inability to pass a message along. It wouldn't have been the first time that it had happened in war.

"How good is your German?" she asked me, tentatively.

"It's up to scratch."

"Are you certain about that? Because if it's not, you'll be killing us all."

I let her question linger, until she knew that I wasn't going to answer. I knew full well that one step in the wrong direction could end up in a total massacre. But we didn't have much choice.

"Sorry, old fruit. I would take your place if I could."

"You could, Mike. Here," I said, handing the motorcycle helmet and dust goggles.

"Can't. I'm afraid," he turned his cheek towards me. "Got this, you see. If they see it they'll know that something is up."

In fairness to him, the wound looked deep, where his skin had seemed to part when the German's head had connected with his skin. Even so, I was convinced that it could have passed off as a wound suffered in a motorcycle accident.

"Anyway, leather isn't really my thing. You'll look far better in it than I would."

"You rotter," I muttered back at him, with a smile on my face. Our falling out had been momentary. Now that we had a new agenda, Mike was back to his old self. I, on the other hand, was still feeling rather fragile.

Mike began convening his men together, instructing them this way and that. A group of men quickly began to dig around the five caltrops that we had buried, while another went to source some dirt from the ditch, ready to fill the craters in the road.

"I want two men further up the road," I said, looking southwards. "When the cars are heard, I want a warning."

"Good call," said Mike, as he pulled two rifle-wielding Frenchmen from the pack, sending them off on their way.

"And make sure you stay up on the bank!" I called out after them as they began their jog to meet the *Generalfeldmarschall*.

"Right, come on then *Herr* Pelletier, let's get you all ready then," Mike chuckled heartily as he began to walk away from me, and back towards the treeline that we had been hiding in recently.

The German motorcyclist was further into the woods than where we had been hiding, now tied to a tree in nothing but his underwear; a thin white top with long Johns to match. He looked quite cold, but that did not really matter too much to us now.

He was fastened to the tree by a rope, that cut into his wrists and ankles, but only on account of how much he was insisting on wriggling. The tree was a good fifty yards or so away from the top of the bank, which meant that, by the time that he realised what was going on behind him, it would be too late for him to shout a word of warning to his comrades.

But I was sure that the rifle that was pointed at him would have more than sufficed.

He looked over at me, disappointed that I hadn't proved as weak as I must have looked. His face turned to one of utter disgust, as he realised that he had been stripped for one purpose; to clothe me.

I pulled his uniform on over me, his eyes falling longingly on the clothes that I left in a pile on the floor. Underneath his uniform, I kept a thin shirt on, so that I would, when the impending confusion commenced, be able to take off the German uniform, and avoid being shot at by people on my own side.

It was a risky manoeuvre, but it was one that had to be done. It was a risk that I considered worth taking, although I wished that someone else could have taken up the baton.

I pulled his boots on with a grimace, as I realised that the German was quite enjoying the fact that I was a good two or three boot sizes larger than he was. My toes, curled up against the extremes of the leather, screamed at me to get them off, to give them some sort of breathing space, but I ignored them.

It had taken me long enough to get them on, to take them off again would simply be a waste of precious time.

Finally, the big, heavy leather overcoat was pulled on over the top of everything else, its double-breasted tunic buttoning all the way up to my neck and stopping just short of my shins. It covered almost every inch of me, and I could imagine how well it felt to the motorcycle owner, particularly when it was bitterly cold outside.

But I was not going to get the chance to test its abilities on the saddle of a bike. In fact, the bike that I was using wasn't going to be going anywhere at all.

"Very fetching," Mike quipped, as he passed an MP40 and the helmet to me. "It suits you. Have you ever considered becoming a Nazi?"

"No, I hear the pay is lousy and the food is bad."

"Is that right?" Mike joked, turning to the German for some sort of an answer. Unsurprisingly, there was not even a flicker of approval behind the hatred that was in his eyes.

Mike came in close to me and began brushing dirt off my collar with the back of his hand. "Yes, quite dashing," he remarked again, before licking his thumb and rubbing on my cheek. "Come here, Jean. What's this all over you?" he said, mockingly.

I pushed him away, chuckling.

"Give over, would you?" I snickered. "Who do you think you are? My mother?"

"I might as well be, the amount of times I end up looking after you."

"Put the helmet on," Suzanne intervened, unimpressed with the level of joviality this close to a contact with the enemy.

I did as I was told, the steely glare reminding me quickly of how most men that we had met had some sort of innate fear of her.

"You forgot this," she said, pulling in close to me and wrapping her arms around my waist.

I looked up at Mike, who was already pulling a mocking face, one of surprise and embarrassment.

Her head came up no higher than my neck and, as she stood there, I caught a faint hint of roses as a gentle breeze rolled in off the top of her head. But, just as quickly as the breeze had rolled in, she had taken a step back, and I was now the proud owner of a black rubber belt, with a dulled metal buckle at the front.

"They would have noticed that you were missing that straight away. It is a good job that I am here, wouldn't you agree, Michel?"

She looked at Mike, as if she knew full well the kind of face that he had been pulling behind her back. Mike didn't answer, but instead flashed a bright shade of red instead.

I shook my head at him and laughed, whispering in his ear as I passed.

"I may not trust her. But she's growing on me all the time!"

He sulked around for a few moments, as if he really didn't like being humiliated by someone like Suzanne. Or maybe it was because she had made it blatantly obvious that he wasn't exactly her type. That sort of thing always had the knack of winding him up.

"Now what?" he said, as he came to join me in the ditch at the side of the road.

"Well," I said, looking up and down the track, at the heads that bobbed around in the ditches on either side. "Now, we wait."

"What's the time?" he asked, his fingers drumming repeatedly on his thigh.

"Quarter to eleven, Mike. Calm down, will you."

"What?"

"You're so tense I can see it."

"Sorry."

He spent the next ten minutes biting down on his lip, hard, his eyes closed as he tried to meditate his way to relaxation. But none of it seemed to be working.

For the life of me I couldn't quite work out what he had to be so uptight about, I was the one doing all the heavy lifting. His remit had barely changed from the original plan. Step out in front of the *Generalfeldmarschall* and pull the trigger a few hundred times.

That was the easy bit.

Just as I was beginning to feel comfortable in the leather ensemble of the German motorcyclist, I heard a scurry of feet behind me. I turned to see a Frenchman scrabbling down the bank, his eyes bulging and mouth wide.

By the time he got to me and Mike, he barely had enough oxygen left in his lungs to speak.

"They're here. They are coming."

"Excellent. How many vehicles?"

"Two cars. Three motorcycles."

"Doesn't sound so bad," Mike chimed. "Maybe things are going to go our way this time."

"One of the motorcycles has a sidecar," the Frenchman added, after sucking in an inhuman amount of air. "With a machinegun."

"Why do you have to open your big mouth?" I said with a grin.

"I did warn you didn't I? I'm cursed. I'm telling you," Mike replied, his voice sticking to the thick air around us.

"Oh, do give it a rest," I muttered, as I pulled myself up from the ditch, every limb aching as if I had just run a marathon. "You're not the one who has found himself wearing this."

Without looking back, I heaved myself into the road, defying all logic and reason, to go and stand directly in front of the oncoming convoy of vehicles and heavy weaponry.

I stood next to the BMW, running my hand over the seat and handlebars, as if I was trying to draw some kind of comfort out of it. It had been kicked up onto its stand, which took just enough weight off the two tyres to enable it to balance where it was.

The front tyre was drooped and deflated, hanging on for dear life.

But then, my attention was drawn elsewhere, away from the bike completely, no matter how much I enjoyed looking at it.

Ahead, I could hear the rumble of engines, this time not just the higher-pitched engine of a motorcycle, but a deeper, more guttural noise, that could only come from a car.

My heart beats quickened. My breathing shallowed. This was it; this was what I had trained for.

All those months of learning about French customs, French clothes and vehicles. All that time spent learning about different explosives and methods of hiding in plain sight. And there I was, standing head on to a convoy of German vehicles, dressed as one of them.

I could make out the two headlights of motorcycles at the front of the group, mercifully not streaks ahead of the cars like I had imagined. I could only pray that the two motorcycles leading the pack were the unarmed ones, and that my chances of receiving a machinegun round to the chest were slimmer than they would be.

From behind the two motorcycle engines, I could make out the headlights of a car, slightly brighter than the motorbikes, and not quite as restricted by the tape.

Perks of being a high-ranking officer, I supposed.

The engines grew louder until they no longer presented themselves as individual growls, but as one cacophony of noise, like a stampede of horses' hooves in the Grand National.

Everything in my body seemed to slow, apart from my heart, as they drew closer. My palms began to sweat, seeping into the leather gloves that I now wore. My brow furrowed, as I questioned whether I really needed to do this.

But, by the time I had the thought, it was already too late.

I breathed out sharply. Then I leant over to the motorbike.

I flicked the headlights on and off. Then again. And a third time for good measure.

The convoy began to slow to a halt.

27

I caught a flash of hair just over to my left, resisting the temptation to look over in Suzanne's direction. If they suspected that someone else was with me, then I would get a bullet in me quicker than I had hoped.

"*Was ist los?*" called out a voice, their faces silhouetted by the headlight beams behind them. As he spoke, brakes squealed to a halt a few yards to the rear. It was all perfect, we had them exactly where we wanted them.

I needed to buy a few more seconds of time, in the hope that they all bunched together just a little bit more, which would make our job much easier.

"Mein Reifen ist geplatzt. Muss einen Stein getroffen haben."

I put on my best German accent, trying to pronounce every single syllable as they would have done, without overdoing it too much. There had been stories of spies wandering into shops up and down the country, only given away by their upper-class British accent, that did not seem to match their appearance nor their surroundings.

I could only hope that I had pulled it off.

There was a moment of silence, where the bike riders turned to one another, discussing what the best plan of action would be.

Then, a call from behind, from one of the cars, most likely asking what the holdup was, the *Generalfeldmarschall* was tired, and wanted to get to bed.

The voice that had called out to me replied, telling them that some fool had managed to burst his front tyre, and needed help getting it back to the Château.

All the while, I kept my hand on the seat of the motorcycle, the pistol grip of the MP40 resting easily under my palm. It was out of sight to them, ready to swing into action at a moment's notice.

I had not hidden it because they weren't expecting me to have a weapon, they more than likely were, but I wanted it somewhere close by, somewhere considerably easier to bring to bear if I was suddenly caught out.

I had my escape route planned already; pull the MP40 up into the aim and squeeze off a few rounds, manoeuvring behind the bike for a bit of additional cover. It would not be a long-term solution, as the petrol tank would be incredibly close to my face, but I hoped that it would be enough for the others to begin replying to help me out.

A voice growled into the darkness ahead of him,

his face far darker than all the others it seemed as if the blackness of the night was attracted to him somehow.

"Bah," he bellowed, as if frustratingly clearing his throat. "*Sag ihm, er soll in mein Auto steigen.*"

Sag ihm, er soll in mein Auto steigen.

I couldn't quite believe what I was hearing, and for a moment I wondered if I had heard correctly.

If I *had* heard correctly, then it would change things.

The rest of those who were with me, wherever they were in the ditches or up on the ledge of the forest, would have to adapt. And they would need to adapt, pronto. Otherwise I would end up dead.

"*Steig in das erste Auto. Wir bringen Sie zurück.*"

I had heard correctly. Things were about to change. They would have to adapt, pronto.

Get in the first car. We will take you back.

I breathed out gently, trying to compose myself for what was about to happen. Timing was now everything. I would have to kick this whole thing off, as close to the *Generalfeldmarschall* as I could dare, but not so late that the convoy would be moving again. If that happened, I really was in it, up to my neck.

Another voice called out to me, with words along the lines of, "Hurry! We haven't got all night," just with a lot more profanity. It was fair enough; the night was beginning to chill and this much inactivity always led to the night time air beginning to bite at your skin.

I grabbed the MP40, passing the sling over my head so that it dangled at my waist. I let it hang there, bashing against my thighs as I gingerly walked over to them. I wanted to be as unthreatening as I possibly could.

They had no reason to believe that I was an enemy, but if I approached them with my finger on the trigger, then it was bound to ring alarm bells. It was akin to a dog approaching his master, head bowed in submission.

I scuffled my way towards the vehicles, trying to take short, slow strides, without them cottoning onto the fact that I was trying to buy some time. I needed Mike and Suzanne to come up with an alternative plan, one that would mean that I wouldn't be caught in the crossfire. But right now, it seemed impossible that I would avoid it.

There was an almost inhuman urge to want to look to my left and right, to find the heads bobbing around there that would tell me that I was not alone. But, knew that even if I did look, I would not see them. Their heads would be pressed firmly into the ditch that they lay in, listening to what was going on above them.

It was only when Mike gave the command that they would make themselves known, and I hoped in the most dramatic of fashions possible.

I nodded to the two motorcyclists who led the column, their engines idling and itching to move on. They seemed nervous, anxious almost to get back and, if I had not been mistaken, wary that something was about to happen.

But they were both young and, I supposed, that the prospect of looking after a *Generalfeldmarschall* was not one that was at the top of every new recruit's to-do list.

Everything in the forest suddenly went quite still. The column of vehicles was stationary, but so too were the occupants. I could not sense any kind of movement from my left or my right, and it felt like even the wildlife in the forest had come to a standstill, all so that I could get a better look at *Generalfeldmarschall* Sperrle.

He was a rotund man, with a face that seemed to sag downwards under the weight. As the headlights behind him continued to shine, it was difficult to pick out too many features of his, but I could see that where he should have eyes, there was nothing more than two black holes. It was as if he was some spectral being.

The gold braiding on his shoulders told me that, even if he wasn't our man, he would be a jolly good replacement. The royal blue uniform was smart, presentable, with another pair of eagles on his collars, to denote how important he truly was.

Medal ribbons seemed to drip from his chest and the Iron Cross that adorned his breast pocket took pride of place over the rest of his uniform. It was impossible to have accrued so many gallantry medals in this war alone, so I concluded that he must have been some kind of flying ace during the last war. Either that or all of the medal ribbons were fabricated, to make it seem that anyone with an ounce of power in the *Reich*, were also true heroes of the Fatherland.

Either possibility seemed plausible.

"*Steig ein. Steig ein,*" he muttered, motioning me to get into his vehicle and sit where his leather briefcase had been placed.

I did as I was told and swallowed hard. I was sitting directly next to the very man that we had been told to kill.

There was, all of a sudden, a thickness to the air around me, quite unlike anything that I had experienced before. It was difficult to take anything in, as if the oxygen had turned into some kind of thick soup.

My heart quickened further. My palms perspired more. But my breathing remained controlled. I knew what was about to happen, and there was nothing I could do about it at all.

Suddenly, my consciousness seemed to fade, the visions that overtook me grabbing a hold of my attention like never before.

Henry was cradled in my arms again, as the search party in Peldon Avenue had continued.

Grace's face came into view, powdered by the brick dust that she had caked on her face. Her face still looked as pretty as it had been five years' before, when I had met her for the first time.

Never would I have imagined that so soon I would be attending her funeral service.

I was fortunate. I had a body, bodies, to bury.

When I died, as I inevitably would do on that night, my parents would have nothing to bury. I would be slung in a heap, with the others who would die with me, with little time for pomp or ceremony.

But there was a part of me that quite liked the idea. At least I wouldn't be alone for eternity. At least I would have died trying to make things right.

As I looked at the rat-faced man sitting next to me, his questions going straight over my head, I imagined how he could have been the one to order the parachute mines to have been dropped on Richmond that night.

"Peldon Avenue," I suddenly heard him shout, smacking the map next to him with his polished oak stick. "Make sure you get Peldon Avenue."

There was a sickness to my stomach as I came to. The *Generalfeldmarschall* continued to stare at me, as he awaited an answer, which he was never going to get. It was almost as if he knew that something was about to happen, as I felt his whole body tense as if hardening himself to attempt to repel any rounds.

I kept my hands firmly away from the MP40, and I toyed with the idea of throttling the man. He had killed my wife. He had killed my son.

Our eyes connected for the first time, his head turned slightly towards me and away from the headlights. I could see into his eyes, which seemed to have no colour. They were simply black little holes, that saw everything.

He began to breathe deeply, his hot breath warming a small part of my face, which made the rest of it burn with a chill. I could smell what he had had for dinner. Some kind of fish, I was sure of it. But I could also taste the wine that he had consumed, bottle after bottle of it, to the point where his bulbous, grotesque nose had begun to redden.

Slowly, deliberately, I reached into my jacket pocket, and I watched as his beady little eyes grew wide at what I was doing. But still, he did not call out to any of his men, he did not scream for his life.

Why would he? I was only a German soldier with a punctured tyre after all.

I gripped my hand around it, firmly, but not too firmly, and withdrew it.

I shook the little cardboard box underneath his nose, as I watched him relax into his seat. I flicked the box open and let him draw a cigarette.

Putting one into my own mouth, I slid the box back into my pocket and reached for the heavier, more robust item that I had in there.

Unfortunately for the *Generalfeldmarschall*, I did not have a light for him. But what I did have was an 1892 *Modele* revolver, six eight-millimetre rounds all sitting in the chamber, just itching to get out.

His eyes traced my movements as I pulled it out fully and aimed it towards his chest. He knew what that meant. One wrong move now and he would have his insides splattered all over the lovely upholstery of the Mercedes-Benz.

I slid the loading gate forward and felt a soft *clink* as the hammer was reengaged. Now, all I had to do, was squeeze the trigger. Just once should do it.

To my right, I heard one of the motorcycle engines begin to scream, ready to move off. But then, a shout. A clamour of urgent bodies. And a gunshot.

28

The gunshot rippled through the air, as a stone does when it plonks into a pond.

There was a thump, as the first motorcycle rider went down, landing in a heap on the floor.

For a second or two, nobody dared to move. It felt like maybe the motorcycle rider was faking it or had some sort of a seizure.

But there had definitely been a gunshot.

Then, there was a roar of engines, as the car behind us, as well as the two remaining motorcycles, closed ranks around the one that they were meant to be protecting with their lives.

Everyone in my car though, had frozen. No one did a thing. But, if they did, they were doing it incredibly slowly.

I eased my breathing back down to normal, as I turned to face Sperrle, pulling the hammer back on the revolver as I did so. Thumbing back the hammer allowed the trigger to tilt back slightly, ready to fire.

All that it would take now would be a slight squeeze on the curved steel and the hammer would be free to fall onto the round, ejecting it and sending it straight into the ugly man's chest.

The need to thumb the hammer backwards in this situation was not all that necessary, but it made the rotund man aware that my intentions were very much real. Lightening the load with which I would have to pull the trigger, meant that I would be able to fire with a greater accuracy, as the moving parts and pressure involved was less. But, when you're sitting inches from your target, if you miss, then you deserve to die. It was as simple as that.

So, I wasn't taking any chances.

Behind the *Generalfeldmarschall's* head, I caught sight of the final motorcycle, making its way to the front of the column, the occupant of the sidecar readying the MG34 that he had at his disposal. Things were about to get very noisy indeed.

I saw that he had a *Patronentrommel*, feeding his weapon, which meant that he would be able to fire seventy-five rounds before he would have to reload. I wondered if he would need to at all, and whether or not they carried spare ammunition in these convoys.

A few flashes from the ditches on either side of the motorcycles told me everything that I needed to know. I wasn't on my own. And it was showtime.

As if the curtain had been lifted on the most

uproarious encore of all time, weapons seemed to burst from all around the tree line, some mixed with flaring tracer rounds, that carved the sky like fireflies.

I had the most important job of all. I was to execute this man who was now sitting in front of me, his terrified eyes bulging like snooker balls.

I squeezed the trigger, waiting for the kickback in my hand and the splattering of blood over my face. But it didn't come. It wouldn't come.

There was something stopping me, as I stared into his bulging eyes, that told me not yet, but maybe not at all.

I was frightened about what I would become if I pulled the trigger. If I killed him, bits of his body would be on me, seeping into the pores of my skin and the fabric of my being.

If I pulled the trigger, then I would be no better than the wolves that he sent over in bombers to decimate and carve the city of London. If I pulled the trigger, I would be no better than him.

There was movement to my right. I turned just in time to see the passenger in the front of the car swivel round to his superior, pistol drawn and ready to throw his body in the way of harm.

He caught sight of the revolver that was pressed into Sperrle's body and shouted.

"Hey!"

I reacted. I spun in my chair and squeezed the trigger, lightly, but enough. The hammer fell and the man's neck suddenly seemed to explode at the artery, as if the pressure had been building for some time.

Warm, sticky liquid showered itself over my face, just as I caught sight of the driver, himself showered in blood, turn to face me, totally weapon-less.

I watched his head, veins throbbing against the side of his skull, as he reached for his comrade's weapon. It was the last thing that he ever did.

I squeezed the trigger, twice, quickly, the driver's head obliterated by two rapid rounds; one to the cheek, the other around his temple. Clumps of smashed skull and bloody tissue clung to the windscreen in front of him, his hand still reaching for the pistol that his friend had drawn out not ten seconds ago.

I had no time to think about what was happening, as suddenly there was a great weight on top of my shoulders, pushing me down towards the footwell of the car.

Sperrle's snarling lips reminded me of a hungry bear, that had been starved for days and was finally getting a hint of sustenance. The man was heavy, but not exactly agile, and he struggled to manoeuvre his mammoth hands around my neck, but wriggling around, he eventually got them there.

He pressed down hard on my throat, as if every inch of his energy had been focused on my windpipe.

Stars began appearing in my eyes, as I realised, I was slowly losing this battle. His upper body pressed down hard on mine, as I tried to manoeuvre my finger back onto the trigger. Even if I had been able to get my finger there, there was no guarantee that the round I managed to fire would harm him at all. It was just as likely to bury itself into *my* guts as it was into his.

But, alas, my fingers were completely immobile, as the numbness began to set in. My limbs, had they been able to, would have flopped, as my body's only focus became about keeping me alive, keeping me conscious.

My head was now pounding in pain, as my brain screamed out for oxygen, from anywhere that it could get some. My nostrils were flared and mouth wide, as saliva and phlegm fought to keep me from dragging in anything that I could use.

All I could see now was his blackened, rat-like eyes, as they began to light up at the prospect of taking me off the earth.

But the man was impatient and, as he tried to finish me off with one final, almighty squeeze, he lifted off my legs to get even more of his plentiful bodyweight behind it.

I didn't need a second chance. With all my might and allowing part of my brain to shut down in the process, I lifted my heavy leg up, into his groin, fast.

It had the desired effect.

He did not lose his grip entirely, but it loosened enough for me to be able to fight back.

Taking a leaf out of the German's book, I launched my head up, into his face, not really caring where I connected with Sperrle's. He howled out in pain as I felt my skull crack onto a tooth, splitting my head and filling his with blood. The headache intensified, to an almost intolerable level, but I knew that if I stopped now, there would be no hope for me whatsoever. It was now or never. He had to be finished off at that moment.

As he leant back, howling like a wounded animal, I fumbled around for the revolver, which I thought had been sandwiched between my chest and his. But it was nowhere to be found.

For half a second, I panicked. But then, I managed to compose myself and remembered the plethora of other ways that we had been taught to kill a man.

I had no time to search for my own weapon, so realised that I would have to improvise.

"Use whatever method you can, to kill your target," the vague Scottish tones reminded me as I sat in the footwell of the car. "But my recommendation would be to use whatever weapon they might be pointing at you."

The Scottish instructor's advice had been sound. But not totally relevant in my case. The *Generalfeldmarschall* had no weapon to speak of, not from what I could see anyway, but his adjutant had.

Kicking his giant weight off me for a moment, using the remaining energy that I had, I hoisted myself up and lunged into the front seat.

I grabbed the pistol, an FN 1910, which the adjutant gladly gave up.

I flicked the safety down and away from the top of the weapon, pulling back the receiver as I did so. I didn't like to waste rounds, but right now I needed to know that there was something in there and ready to fire.

It was a small weapon, almost like a toy gun, and I knew that I would need to place quite a few rounds into Sperlle's body to bring him down, especially as he was such a large figure.

But, as I went to turn, I felt something grip me on the ankles, clamping onto and dragging me back down.

I fell onto the backseat of the car, just as the MG34 began to spark up ahead of us. It didn't seem that any of the other soldiers were aware of what was happening in the car. They were far too preoccupied with all the other figures who had suddenly emerged from the shadows.

I scrabbled around, hoisting myself up to lean on my elbows, to make sure that I watched the man die as I pulled the trigger. But there was a problem. There was already a weapon in front of me. It was the *Modele* 1892 revolver.

Part of me was entertained by the thought of being killed by the very weapon that had been mine. But the other part of me was distraught that I was going to die in this way; shot on the back seat of a German staff car, having had more than ample opportunity to pull the trigger on the man who was now bearing down on me.

There was no hope. There was no chance of the 1892 failing to fire. It had three rounds left in the cylinder and I could practically see one of the rounds lining up with the barrel, I was that close to it.

From behind the weapon, the snarling face of the *Generalfeldmarschall* returned, blood pouring from his mouth, and a nice bruise forming on his swollen face.

There was nothing I could do, apart from point the meagre looking weapon at his chest, so we were at a stand-off.

The world around me seemed to go quite still, as if every creature had ceased to do anything, out of amazement at what was happening in the car.

The first one to squeeze the trigger would be the winner, but both of us seemed reluctant to do so.

I could see the cogs whirring behind his eyes. He was going to try and ride this one out. If he could, then there was a chance that he could take me in, interrogate me and bleed as much information from my brain as he could, before disposing of me.

But it was all wishful thinking. He clearly hadn't seen how many we outnumbered him by.

And, judging by the silence of the MG34, we now outgunned them too.

We stared straight at each other for what felt like hours, as I sensed his finger gradually applying the pressure to the curved steel of the trigger. It was only a matter of seconds away now; I could feel it. I could only hope that if I was the first to take the hit, that I would have enough life left in my body to pull the trigger as I fell.

The *Generalfeldmarschall's* shoulder suddenly erupted, a spout of blood shooting up towards the heavens, taking his gold-braided shoulder patch with it. Then, his face seemed to explode in a similar fashion, as a round went straight through the side of his cheek.

He stared at me in utter disbelief, his lower face seemingly disconnected from the rest of his body. The round had gone through one side of his cheek, taken out most of his teeth and tongue, and exited through the other side.

But he still wasn't dead.

My right arm suddenly seared with pain, and I felt the round from the 1892 thump gently into the padded leather behind me.

I slumped backwards, just in time to watch as his chest burst open, with the accuracy of a surgeon's knife, before he too, slumped backwards.

His rat-like eyes stared up into the inky blackness above him.

29

“Why does it always seem to be me that’s saving you?” Mike said, as he offered an outstretched hand.

“Because I’m the one who does all the real work,” I replied, spitting out a few broken teeth and more than a little bit of blood.

“You alright?” he asked me, gently wiping his hand over my arm.

“Tickety-boo,” I replied, as he pulled me down beside the car.

The MG34 had sparked up again, which confirmed that these boys had come packed and ready for a fight. Rounds thudded into the other side of the car, one or two of them passing through the sides and hitting the interior quite hard.

“We need to move from here,” I gasped, as I tried to put the thought of the searing pain out of my mind.

"We can't. We're pinned down by that machinegun here."

"Where are the others?"

"Jerry's managing to keep their heads down, for now. We've only managed to kill one of the motorcycle riders."

I glanced up at him, as he double-checked that his MP40 was all in working order. I had dropped mine somewhere in the car.

"Can you cover me? I need to get back inside the car."

"No, you don't. You'll get peppered in there, Johnny."

"Well, I can hardly fight them with this, can I?" I lifted up the FN 1910 for him to look at. His look said it all; that's going to kill no one.

I pulled the German helmet off my head and stripped down to the layers that made me identifiable to everyone else. It would have been just my luck to escape a close call like that, only to be riddled with holes by someone meant to be on my side.

I pushed the safety back up on the FN and tucked it away in my trousers for safekeeping. I had no idea if it would come in handy again later on.

"You all set?"

He nodded.

"Right then, after three. Three!"

I leapt up, not giving Mike a chance to argue against what I was about to do, but force him into doing what I wanted him to do anyway. He darted to look around the front of the car, and I heard him firing off rounds in bursts of three, to keep the weapon closely trained on its target.

I wrenched the driver's door open, yanking his body out of the way before scrabbling into the back to find my weapon. It was in the footwell, by the body of the *Generalfeldmarschall*, and within seconds it was mine.

The car suddenly began to rock as I felt the headlights disintegrate under the force of the MG34. Mike must have ducked back behind the vehicle, as it rocked further still as the operator swept the gun backwards and forwards, sparks flying everywhere as rounds connected with the dials.

The sustained fire kept on coming, with the stuffing of the leather chairs flying out over my face, as the beautiful leather upholstery was completely decimated. Even the *Generalfeldmarschall* took a few extra rounds, just to be sure.

I lay on my back, my face tightly screwed up, clutching the weapon to my chest, as I let the rounds have their way. I was merely waiting for the inevitable round to strike my body. But it didn't seem to come.

I slid my way through the front of the vehicle, joining Mike back where we had started.

"No chance of using this vehicle to get away then," he quipped, as he fired another three-round burst around the front of the vehicle. He recoiled dramatically as another host of bullets ripped into the grill, the bits of metal twanging and screaming as they were ripped from their mountings.

He began to laugh erratically, as he changed the magazine on his MP40, tucking the empty one down his trousers for later on. We had been taught never to just throw them away. We might come across a whole crate of nine-millimetre ammunition, which would be completely useless if we didn't have anything to put them into. We had been trained to become hoarders.

His laugh was a hollow one, the kind that someone gave when they had just received some awful news, or when they knew that they were about to die. I wondered how he was even managing to shoot straight, there was that much water filling up in his eyes. I could tell he was scared, but he was trying his hardest to plug every hole that was leaking it.

"We better move," he suggested, "Before they realise that they could turn this whole thing into a ruddy great bomb if they wanted to."

He was right. All it would take would be a few, well-aimed rounds towards the petrol tank, and this whole thing would become a charred ruin of twisted metal and singed bodies. We needed to move, and fast.

"Where to?" I asked, poking my eyes just over the top of the car.

"Not sure," he replied, as the roar of a motorcycle engine, thundered at the foundations of the earth. "They're moving the bike!" he began screaming, as the engine was throttled, and the bike began to manoeuvre around.

The machinegun began to open up, as the man in

the sidecar started spraying the entire area with lethal rounds. As he turned, his back opened up to us momentarily and, in unison and without any kind of agreement, both Mike and I lifted our weapons up to our shoulders.

Burying the flimsy stock into my shoulder, I breathed calmly, no ounce of hesitation on my finger this time. I waited for the post of the front sight to line up with the man's body and squeezed.

A nanosecond later, Mike did the same.

We would never know which one of us had been the one responsible for silencing that machinegun, but deep down, we both knew it didn't matter. But that wouldn't stop us arguing for the claim later on.

I emptied another few rounds towards the driver of the bike, who slumped over his handlebars, the throttle slipping, as he sent the corpses charging towards the ditch at the side of the road.

I looked towards Mike, relieved. We were now relatively free to run, apart from the odd round of tracer that zipped into the ground ahead of us.

We threw ourselves into the ditch at the side of the road, shortly to be joined by Suzanne and two other men.

"We have lost about five men," she reported. "But we have only one man left in that car."

"In that case, we should withdraw. Keep some behind to engage with him while the rest retreat. That German isn't going to want to keep poking his head out now he's all on his own."

"No," Suzanne argued, defiantly. We already knew that whatever happened, we had already lost this argument. "We kill every last one of them. We don't want him to be able to report back what happened. It won't take long."

Everything had suddenly calmed, with only a few gunshots ringing out as the clean-up began. Then, the bold, lone German let out three rounds from his pistol, making a throaty echoing sound, as if he was firing into a barrel.

A man, who was foolishly sauntering towards the machinegun, crumpled in a heap on the floor, before wriggling around clutching at his throat, as if he had swallowed a bee.

A volley of shots rang out in retaliation, none of them really anywhere close to hitting their target but peppering the Mercedes nicely as they did so.

A handful of men cautiously moved towards the car, their variety of weapons raised and ready to shoot anything that moved.

The car was suddenly the scene of a ferocious light show, coupled with echoing reports of weapons as they bounced off the nearby trees. If the man wasn't dead before, then he certainly was after twenty rounds of ammunition were emptied into his body at close range.

People began to drag themselves out of the holes that they had burrowed into, inspecting the dead and taking anything that would come in useful to them.

"You need attention on your arm," Suzanne

suggested, taking it in her hands and inspecting it carefully.

"It can wait. We need to leave, now."

As if it had been waiting for my command, a truck suddenly roared from the southern end of the road. It drove with no headlights, only switching them on the second it came to a stop. It was unlike the other vehicles, in that there were no restrictions on its lights, flooding the whole area in an artificial white light.

For a second, we were totally blinded by it. But then, my eyes adjusted, and I could make out the outline of a Blitz truck, the same kind that I had seen back in *Tours* around a week before. It was open-backed and stuffed with as many troops as it could carry.

"How on earth did they get here so quickly?"

Mike looked at me, a panicked look upon his face. He was right. We had only hit the *Generalfeldmarschall's* convoy about two minutes before, and it was a little bit of a coincidence that a fully laden truck should turn up, right on time.

They must have been warned by someone.

We both looked to Suzanne, but she had vanished.

Looking out of the ditch, I just caught her head as it bobbed down into the other ditch on the other side of the road.

It was just as we went to follow her, that the bullets let fly.

There must have been an additional twenty men

now, which, seeing as we had lost at least five already, meant that we were now outnumbered. Two to one.

We scurried backwards, like retreating rats, as the rounds began to thwack into the ditch just ahead of us. There was no way we were going to stay in the barrel and let them shoot at us at will.

We ducked behind the front of the car, seeing for ourselves the true amount of damage that the MG34 had inflicted upon the vehicle it had meant to protect.

The front grill was nothing more than a mash of twisted metal, and the rest of the bonnet had not fared much better either. Mike had taken notice of it too.

"I reckon we could do with some of that right now. What do you say, old fruit?"

"Reckon we can make it?"

"We'll have to give it a go."

The Germans had no cover up their end of the road, apart from using their own truck, which was parked at such an angle that it blocked almost the entirety of the road.

"At least that means they aren't expecting any tanks to join us," I suggested to Mike, as he pointed out the Blitz to me.

He chuckled softly, as he eyed up the bike again, which was facing northwards, and back towards the château.

"I'm worried what they're going to bring from up there," he said morosely.

"Agreed. We need to get rid of as many of this lot as we can, then scarper."

"Let's go for the bike then, and hope they left some rounds for us."

"Sounds like a plan."

"There is one condition though, old fruit," Mike said, a surprising chirpiness to his voice.

"What's that?"

"I get to drive. I've always wanted to drive one of those things."

"That's good. Because I've always wanted to fire one of *those* things," I said, pointing to the MG34.

"Excellent, it seems that we both get our dying wish."

We both paused, for a moment, as Mike realised his poor word choice had scared the two of us. His face broke out into a deep smile.

"Come on then, let's show them what we've got."

We gave a slight grimace, and a nod of appreciation for one another, as we waited for the right opportunity.

The volley of rifle fire seemed to happen in groups of five rounds each, so all we had to do was wait for one of the gaps.

Briefly, there was silence. But, as we emerged from behind the car, the two figures, out in the open, suddenly became the interest of every German weapon in France.

30

There was no mistaking Mike's complete and utter joy that he was about to ride his very first German motorbike. He had been the proud owner of a Vincent Comet, which had seen many a near-miss on the country lanes around RAF North Weald.

That was the problem with young fighter pilots, they came so close to death on a daily basis up in the air, that when they were back on the ground, they thought of themselves as completely invincible. It had led to more than one tragic accident in our short time at Weald. None of which stopped Mike from doing his best to become involved in a high-speed crash.

He seemed to forget completely that we were now under heavy enemy fire, the aim being ever so slightly off, just enough to allow Mike some time to caress the motorcycle and get her purring.

"Cor, would you listen to that!" he exclaimed, as the pulsating feeling rumbled through my backside. It did truly feel wonderful, to be at the mercy of such a powerful machine. It was a feeling that I had missed, one that neither of us had experienced since we had been back in the cockpit of the Hurricanes.

"Never mind that, Mike. We need to get a move on!"

He looked around startled to find that it wasn't just him and the bike. Their love affair was to be brief and ruined by me.

Within a second or two, he had the thing facing the right way and it was now my turn to snap out of the romantic trance that I was in.

I lifted up the feed cover at the top of the gun, and quickly slid the drum magazine off the left-hand side. Flicking the carry handle over to one side allowed me to peer inside it, and I was automatically comforted by the number of rounds that I had at my disposal.

"We should be all good here, Mike," I bellowed, over the roar of the gunfire, as I went about replacing the drum and getting the weapon ready.

There was a sudden *ping* as a round deflected off the front wheel guard, and both Mike and I instinctively ducked down to avoid anything further.

I suddenly had the thought that there wouldn't be too many more of them that evening. I had used up my fair share of close calls now, and the next one would ping me somewhere vital.

"Bring me into range!" I shouted at Mike, and he

dutifully revved the engine and charged towards the enemy, like a valiant knight of the realm.

I felt the air thicken again as we got closer to the truck, before Mike stopped and brought his MP40 off his shoulder and into the aim.

"Go!" I screamed at him, the blood vessels ripping at the back of my throat. "There's no point in the both of us being killed! Go!"

He looked at me in disbelief, or at least I think he did, as I was already too busy staring down the iron sights of the machinegun, preparing to loose off rounds in every direction.

I focused in on two Germans who were using the front cab of the truck as cover, their feet foolishly visible underneath the open door.

My first few rounds were high, smashing into the window and spraying them with glass, but my following burst was spot on, and I could imagine the pain as the rounds ripped into their flesh, exposing shattered bone and muscle.

They both writhed around for a moment, as I kept my gaze on them, until I was satisfied that they weren't going to be getting up in a hurry. They were of no real threat to me, so it was my time to move on.

But, as I did so, I became the attention of every man that was there, including one who had made his way down the ditch at the side of the road and was now taking potshots at me from a matter of yards away.

He began to fumble around with his rifle,

panicking so much that the bolt would not go into its housing that he forgot to take cover as he did so. It was a fatal mistake.

I was sure that I was able to see his heart as he sank back down into the ditch.

I squeezed off another few rounds into the truck, as the heavy wooden stock smashed into my shoulder one time too many. Blood was now gushing through the front of my shirt, the pain reaching an unbearable level.

Just as I felt like giving up, I heard a click.

The truck up ahead of me was now full of holes and shattered glass, the few troops left uninjured were standing well behind the cover of the truck so that I could not get to them.

But I had run out of ammunition. The drum was completely empty. Panicked, I began to look around in the sidecar, my feet sprawling about like a spider's legs, trying to find another drum, or at least a box with some more ammunition in it.

But there was nothing there other than another empty drum. I was spent.

"Jean!" came a cry from the ditch. "Get over here, now!"

There was a burst of gunfire, and the small, inadequate windshield of the motorcycle shattered, splintering my left cheek in fine glass. I felt the blood begin to fall immediately.

The call came again, this time far more urgent,

and with a hint of worry that I was no longer able to hear them.

Ignoring the pain in my arm, that seared as if a branding iron was burning into my flesh, I pushed myself from the sidecar, beginning to run.

Something jumped up from the ground and bit me in the back of the leg, which sent to the floor. The pain was not so bad, at first, and I was able to continue running, before throwing myself face down into the nearest Frenchman that I could find.

He brushed me down, looking into my face like a worried father, before I rolled away from him, to go and find Mike.

"This is hopeless," I breathed, as Mike gripped my shoulder. "We need to fall back, and quickly."

He wasn't focused enough for my liking.

"How do you think they knew? They must have had those soldiers up there ready and waiting for us. Someone talked."

I ignored him, now was not the time for speculation and second-guessing. He would get plenty of time to do that later on.

"Suzanne, order everyone to fall back. We're going to have to risk it."

"No," she answered, with a burning frustration in her eye. "Not until they are all dead."

"Suzanne, there won't be enough of us left to kill them all. They'll just keep sending more men."

"So be it."

I didn't have the energy to fight with her any

longer. I had blood pouring from my arm and my cheek, and my head was still reeling from the contact with the *Generalfeldmarschall's* teeth.

The back of my leg had started to ignite, just like the rest of my wounds, and I felt as though my body was slowly shutting down. I had barely taken a breath in the last ten minutes.

As if my pain wasn't enough, a body suddenly came crashing down on my shoulders, sending my face into the dirt and the wind from my lungs. An apologetic Frenchman shuffled away from me, with eyes like a naughty dog.

"We have got what you asked for," the man said, bringing up a handful of German stick grenades into view. Suzanne grinned.

"You might get your wish, after all, Jean. This should give them a headache at least."

She took two from the man, giving two to another, before whispering in their ears gently. Then, without warning and with only a blast from an MP40 for cover, the man leapt up from the ditch and sprinted to the other side of the road. It was an utter marvel that he had made it that far.

"Michel, Jean. Take the others back, through the forest. This should keep them occupied for the time being. I will see you back at Alfred's place."

We gave her a stern look, one that told her plainly that we were far from happy with the situation.

"He is injured," she insisted. "You should take

him back and get him seen to. You will need a head start at least."

"And what are you planning on doing? You hardly have any ammunition left."

"Those men are crawling up to the Germans, we will keep them busy for now. When they are close enough, they'll throw the grenades under the truck. That way, we hope to make a big explosion."

It seemed sound enough, but she hadn't exactly factored in that the men might be spotted long before they ever got to their target.

And then there was the small problem of actually throwing the grenades. It was a nice weapon to have in the arsenal, but it was fiddly to use, especially if you were that close to the enemy. And a scared man's hands always shook.

They would first have to remove the screw lid at the bottom of the wooden handle, which would allow a small ball to fall out of the end. Pulling down on that sharply would ignite the fuse, using friction, which in turn would then burn until it reached the detonator. And when it reached the detonator, well, you wouldn't want to be anywhere near the thing.

But these men were doing it, trying to stay concealed all the time, and by the time the first one had gone off, the second would be ready to throw which, if they were unfortunate, would mean all the surviving Germans would be on the lookout for them.

"Just trust me, would you?" she said, in response to the concerned look on our faces.

Mike exchanged a glance with me, just in case I was in any doubt about where he thought he could place his trust.

"Alright," I conceded.

"But—"

"Michel, we have done what we came here to do. We will be better served if we survive and continue to make contact in London. These men know what is expected of them. We should be aware of what London expects us to do."

He knew that I was right, even though he refused to acknowledge it in any way.

I knew that, whatever happened, if I was to leave that ditch, he would follow me. He had no other option.

"We will put down some covering fire for you. *Bon chance.*"

We returned the good fortune, before making a run for it, in a hail of bullets.

31

"I heard there was a disturbance in the night last night," Alfred said, as he shuffled in with a tray of tea and buttered bread. "Some group tried to kill a high-ranking *Luftwaffe* officer."

"Were they successful?" I asked, catching Mike's eye.

"If the Germans are to be believed, then no, they weren't. But they seem pretty angry everywhere. And if not angry, then scared. I've never seen so many of them carrying their guns off their shoulders around here."

"Do they have any idea who did it?"

"No, but I have heard a name."

"Oh?"

"Fortunae."

He gave us a slight smile, as he surrendered even more of his hospitality to us.

"Did you sleep alright last night, my friends?" he asked with another, wry smile on his face.

"Yes, most wonderfully. Thank you."

"Good. Good," he replied as he slid into his chair, taking a large mouthful of his tea, followed by a sigh. He looked towards the photograph on top of the mantlepiece.

"He would have been proud," he said, with a tone of triumph to his voice.

"Of what, Alfred?"

"I don't think he would have ever imagined that his father would have been the host of two cut-throat murderers." At the mention of the boy, his ornate handkerchief was withdrawn.

"We're not murderers," I begged, with a sweeping smile.

"Assassins then. Is that any better?"

"Thank you for the tea, Alfred."

If only I had known that it was the last time that I would ever see him, I would have thanked him for a whole load of other things besides.

The End

Rejoin Johnny Parker and Michael Hope in 'Playing with Fire,' now available on Amazon.

ALSO BY THOMAS WOOD

Gliders over Normandy:

The Silent Invader

All Men are Casualties

As If They Were My Own

The Trench Raiders:

Slaughter Fields

Wavering Warrior

Invisible Frontline

Take Aim

Clouded Judgement

Long Forgotten

Alfie Lewis Thrillers:

The Evader

The Executioner

The Betrayed

Circuit Fortunae:

Don't Look Back

Playing with Fire

Close Quarters

www.ingramcontent.com/pod-product-compliance
Lightning Source LLC
Chambersburg PA
CBHW021620030826
48979CB00034B/491

* 9 7 8 1 9 1 6 4 1 3 8 5 6 *